APOLOGY

This is a book with two Indigenous main characters. I honestly do not know if I have any Indigenous genes in me or not, I apologize for writing this book. It took a few years to write, and I had it in mind before that.

I only know that I have often been mistaken for being Indigenous, because of how I look. I have very dark hair and eyes, sort of dark skin that tans coppery, my eyes slant, and I have high cheekbones. Often, it is Indigenous people thinking that I am. I have even been accused of "Passing for White", and of "Denying my heritage".

It can be very confusing. My family has no official records of any Indigenous ancestors. My brother has been doing our family tree for decades, and never found any. Also, his Ancestry DNA test showed none. I found from Ancestry's videos that it might not show up in all siblings, so I plan to get a DNA test when I can afford one.

I have done research on Indigenous culture online, and have taken two courses. One from The University of Alberta, and one from OISE at University of Toronto.

Again, I apologize for writing this, and for any mistakes in what my characters think or do.

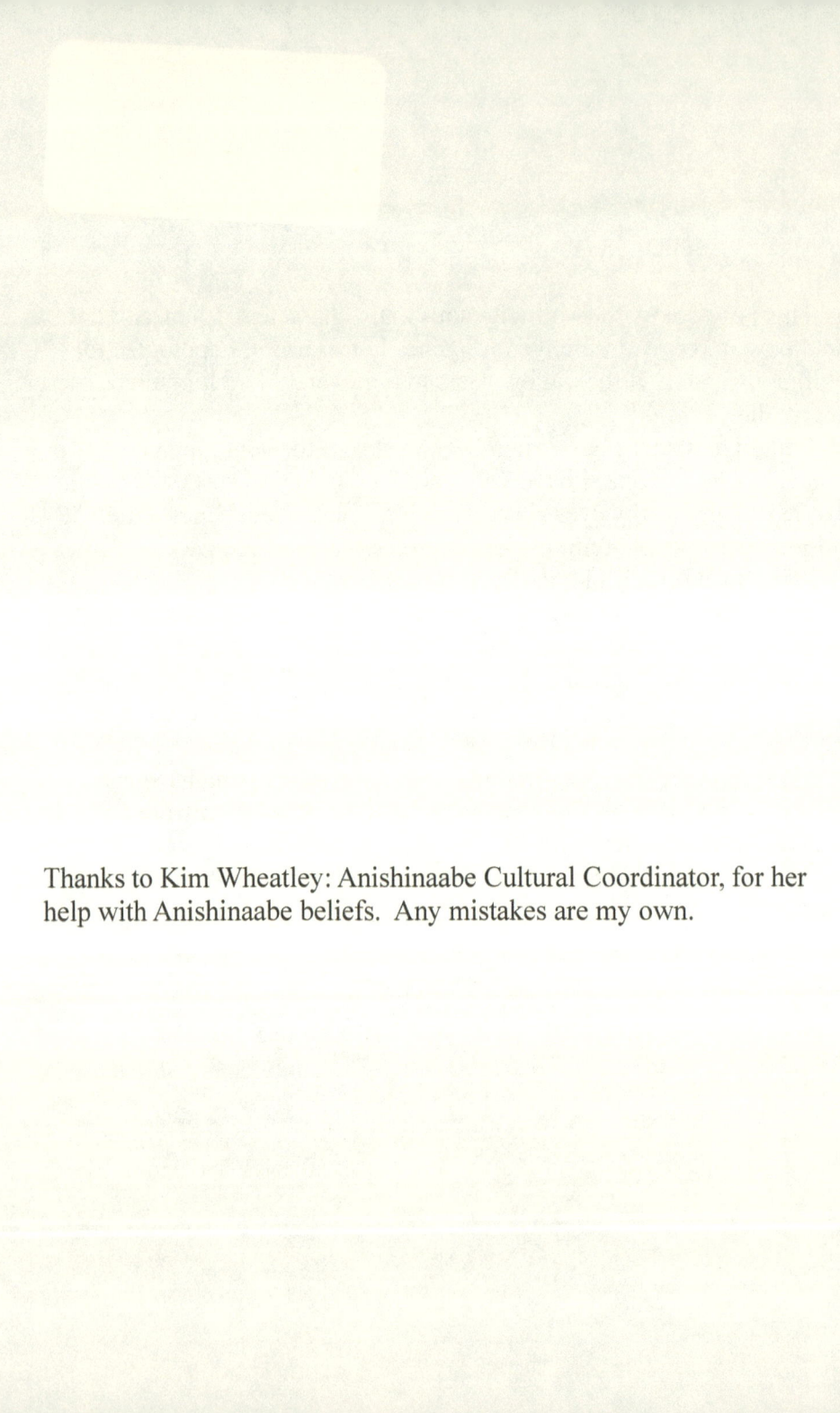

Thanks to Kim Wheatley: Anishinaabe Cultural Coordinator, for her help with Anishinaabe beliefs. Any mistakes are my own.

In memory of Nik Beat, poet, writer, helper of artists.

Prologue

Aiyana was fed up. They wanted her to to send souls to Hell! What for? For being so poor and uneducated that the person had had to turn to prostitution? For doing drugs out of despair? She had been picked and trained for that? She refused to do it.

Quietly, she had been letting such souls go into the light. Soon, though, she could be found out. That would lead to punishment in solitary, and after that, she would never be left alone. All for disobeying terrible Orders. It was bad enough, being a woman in the overly strict Arrows of God, but she would have it even worse if caught. Also, Aiyana no longer wanted to be part of their prejudiced religion. She had been stolen from her real family at a very young age, she believed. She needed to find her own culture.

She had to leave. Now.

For months, she had been searching for ways to escape them, and where to go. She had found out, that in Canada, there were not many Arrows of God. There were just a few street corner missionaries, with no established churches.

In Toronto, Canada's biggest city, she could easily disappear. Many races of people lived there. She wouldn't stand out as being too different.

So...tonight, Aiyana (known as 'Agnes' by The Arrows), would escape. And hunt for a secretive group that was good to spirits, and against what The Arrows of God did.

Tonight.

Chapter One

The railway car creaked and rattled. It was dark and stuffy. Piles of boxes filled every corner. The wind howled through its cracks like a banshee. Even though Aiyana had known many ghosts, it still was a bit frightening.

Aiyana huddled in a corner, shivering. She should have brought a blanket! Time went by slowly, as she worried about finding a safe place to live in Toronto, and about getting off of the train secretly. She had no passport, nor any I.D.

Amidst the moans, clicks and wailing wind, she thought that she heard faint cries. Could it be a cat, meowing? Stiffly, she got up to investigate.

Behind some highly stacked boxes, a woman lay, gasping. In her arms, a small black kitten huddled. A stench of vomit, bad wine, and some sort of drug surrounded the woman. Her bruised arm had a needle sticking out of it.

As Aiyana came closer, the woman's face seemed to blur, as cat features rippled across it. Her arms spasmed on the kitten, who mewed softly. Gently, Aiyana took away the kitten, and the woman opened up her eyes.

"Bad stuff. I---think--I think I'm a goner..." she gasped. "Take care -- my baby..." she heaved another breath, as her clouded eyes pleaded.

"Of course. I love cats."

"She's not quite..." the woman gasped out, as Aiyana could see her spirit pulling out of her body. The kitten looked up, and seeing the spirit, mewed softly. She held onto Aiyana with...what _were_ they? It seemed to be small, furry—_hands?_ Aiyana cuddled the kitten more closely.

Suddenly, the spirit's voice sounded loudly in her head.

"Oh no! You're one of those _Arrows!_"

"NO! Not anymore! I'm escaping from them! Do you need help into The Light?"

"I'd like to stay, and watch over my baby," the hovering spirit softly said, looking with love at the kitten.

"Your baby?"

"I was a cat when I got pregnant," the spirit seemed to actually blush. Then, she grinned suddenly. "It sure was fun! Wild! Now, she is both...I don't know if she will be able to turn human."

Aiyana looked into the blue kitten eyes, wondering. The kitten seemed contented now, with her mother hovering by her.

"She is old enough to not need my milk, but I couldn't let her go on her own," the spirit continued.

"Or give up the drugs, it seems," Aiyana muttered. Aloud she said, "Could she be addicted, too?"

"I had stopped just before getting pregnant. Being a cat helped. Today, I just needed one last fix..." the spirit sighed. She and Aiyana looked sadly at the motherless kitten/baby. The spirit rose, and drifted a bit around the rail car, seeming thoughtful.

"You said that you were escaping from The Arrows?" she asked.

"Yes, I am escaping from them."

"Why couldn't you just walk out? Are they that hard to leave?"

"I am too good with spirits for them to let me leave. I was in their main complex, usually watched," Aiyana explained.

"Why leave? Weren't you really rich? The leaders sure are, and you were with them."

"I could NOT send people like you to the Hell realms!! The Arrows are the Evil ones! I was taken from my true family at a very young age. Never saw them again." Tears came to Aiyana's eyes.

"Ahh! I see...Well, then, I'll help you to get into a good place to live in Toronto. Where I was headed. Shape changers in trouble go there. They're very well guarded, and nobody would expect to find someone like you, there!"

"You <u>will</u>?"

"You're taking care of my baby. So, I'll take care of you. She'll be safer there, too. How could a cat with <u>hands</u> survive in most places? Cat adopters could be afraid of her!"

Aiyana closed her eyes in relief. She would have somewhere to stay. A place to hide, among other hiding people.

She went back to her corner, carrying the kitten/baby. The spirit came with her. The body would be found when the car was opened in Toronto. She would slip out past the guards the same way that she had slipped in. Somehow, they never seemed to see her when she thought hard about being unseen.

Chapter 2

Aiyana cuddled the tiny kitten/baby, as she waited close to the car doors. The train screeched on the tracks as it slowed to a stop. The doors were pushed open, and Aiyana lowered herself to a crouch, and quickly stole through them before the workmen looked in. They all were looking the other way, as the woman's spirit made odd noises. She rushed into the shadows of the train platform. Behind her, she then heard shouts as the body was found.

The woman's spirit flowed ahead of her on the tracks. Soon, they arrived at Union Station. People flowed around Aiyana, as she made her way through them. Good thing that she had someone to direct her! she thought.

They walked west, and then south. In front of them, Aiyana could see the broken remains of once tall buildings. Now, a mass of broken glass, and rusted metal rose against the sky. She felt anxious, being back at her vaguely remembered birth place. Leaves and debris now scuttled underfoot. Dust from the broken concrete and rust hurt her eyes and nose. Tears came up. Were they from the dust, fear, or memories? She choked them back, to be able to *see* the ghost leading her to a hopefully safe place.

* * *

Guyan felt great peace encompass him, after sending a spirit into the light. Even though it had been difficult, he had helped save a troubled and trapped soul. It felt good. But his hands tightened into fists, as he thought of those who would force such spirits into darkness and despair. To a place filled with evil entities. Guyan meant to stop this happening. He had so few who could send spirits on, though, and it was hard work for all of them. He needed more help. He needed someone who could easily walk in the spirit worlds.

He carefully breathed in and out, counting his breaths. Breathing out his rage at those who sent the spirits to darkness, so that the soul going off would only feel peace and light as it rose up. He sensed it running to its family, and into a bright light with them.

Guyan gently shut the door. He smiled, thinking of the others that he had saved from pain. It made him more determined to <u>win.</u> To stop Them—those who hated all who were not like themselves.

***

Aiyana could dimly see spirits among the broken towers. She huddled into her thin coat, still hiding the kitten. Would she have to help all of those spirits? Grubby people glared at her from dark doorways. Did she look too prosperous, even in her soiled and thin coat?

An Indigenous man's spirit came up to her, crying out, "I need to go home! Why can't I find it?" Aiyana had to help him.

"Spirit;" she said in her mind, "you are now free from this despair.

Look up into the light."

"What light? I can't see any light!!!" he cried.

"Look at the light!" Aiyana ordered strongly, as she opened up the doorway into the light filled next world. Dust motes sparkled in its bright white light. The scowling doorway people seemed to sense something, and their expressions lightened, and became almost friendly. The spirit finally looked up.

"Buster!" he happily called out.

"WOOF!" A loud bark came from a bulldog that stood in the doorway, and the spirit man ran joyfully to his dog. He gathered the dog into his arms. Then, he turned to Aiyana.

"Thank you, sister." He then went through the door, the dog licking his face. Aiyana shut the door, but kept her head down in her collar.

Her ghost guide looked back at Aiyana, motioning to her to keep following. They soon were at a subway. Nervously, she looked at the people getting on. Were any of them Arrows? Someone with hard eyes stood near a sign. Was he looking at her? Aiyana ducked her head again. Others streamed between them, ignoring the man. The frightening moment passed.

Aiyana began to relax on the subway. It would be harder to find her now. She felt farther and farther away from The Arrows' complex, the more she travelled in Toronto.

The spirit floated down the train, and Aiyana followed her. People engrossed in their phones never looked up. The spirit's voice came to her, "Next stop!" and Aiyana went to wait by the doors. She followed the spirit off of the train. Another step in her way to a new, and a better life. She hoped.

This area had even more broken down buildings. A large area of condo buildings had been emptied, leaving a broken ghost town. People now chose to live in small, friendly neighbourhoods, instead of concrete areas. Toronto's population had gone down, along with the world's. The main refugees to Canada were from the very closed down United States, and not many managed to get away from there. Aiyana was amazed at how easy it had been for her. Could there be some other lucky U.S. Refugees here? Would she want to meet them?

As they passed into the shadows of the old condos, Aiyana shivered. She hoped that she had made the right decision. Cheered by grass and flowers bursting through many cracks in the concrete, she kept going. Her purposeful stride, though, seemed to make her get noticed. Others here seemed to move slowly, and just hang around the corners. This was the home of the homeless, the forgotten and ignored. Perhaps not quite hopeless, she thought, as she saw some sharing their money with others who had even less. It was the best place to hide, she told herself.

"Need a place to stay, little girl?" The slimy voice came from a dark doorway. A pimp, from his overdressed look and tone of voice. Aiyana kept walking. Ahead, there was a far more frightening site: a clean cut young man, with brochures to hand out. He could be from The Arrows of God. Fortunately, her guiding spirit slipped into a dark passageway. Aiyana quickly followed her. The pimp looked actually worried!

"Don't go in there!" he cried out. "There's spooks in there!! and...and..." he stepped towards the passageway, afraid to get too close to it. Aiyana still ran down the alley.

A sweet faced ghost appeared in front of her. "Who are you? Are you one of them?" Her face turned angry, as she advanced on Aiyana. Her spirit friend stepped in between.

"She helps us!" she said. The angry spirit stopped, looking confused.

"Help me, please!" Aiyana blurted out. "The man out there might be after me any minute! I need to hide! Where can I hide?" She looked around frantically, seeing only blank walls. Would the Arrow Church's recruiter be after her down this alley soon? Would he be after these poor spirits, too?

The spirit studied her quietly. "I am Elan," she said. "Don't worry about us here. We protect each other. You seem to have great power. But, we can hide even you!"

"Thank you! Thank you so much!"

Suddenly, many spirits surrounded her. She saw the pimp hurriedly draw back from the mouth of the alley, face greenish and terrified. She did not see the Arrow recruiter at all. Probably he had no ability to interact with spirits.

"We can be seen if necessary," Elan explained. She then looked at Aiyana's ghostly guide. "Who are you?"

"Ava White," she answered. "I was scheduled to move here, but...you can see what happened."

Elan nodded, and just said, "Both of you come with us."

The broken buildings rose around them. Aiyana followed the spirits through the jumbled rubble. Hope sprang into her. It certainly looked like a perfect area to hide in. She silently prayed that the Arrow recruiter hadn't paid much attention to her, and just saw her as a nameless runaway. From the dirty look that he had given her, he had seen her as another runaway.

"Why are you praying?" a voice said in her ear.

"The Arrow man—did he see me?"

"Don't worry. He only notices converts," the spirit said sarcastically.

"Doesn't he try hard to get more converts?"

"Around <u>HERE??</u>" chuckles surrounded her. "They are all too afraid! Of us!" A strange, circular wind blew up, making dust and papers swirl.

Elan drifted back, from the front of the group of spirits. "This way." She gestured to a dark entrance. An archway loomed. Gargoyles at each side seemed to have moving eyes, and looked ready to jump. As Aiyana's eyes widened nervously, Elan said, "Don't worry. It's good inside. The gargoyles protect this place."

"The gargoyles? Aren't they just statues?"

"Not here. Here, they are *alive.*"

Aiyana looked at one of the gargoyles, that was attached to an entrance pillar. A sparkle of green its eyes seemed to look back at her. One eye then slowly winked.

"O—Kayyy...." Aiyana smiled at the feisty gargoyle. Then, green light shot out of the eyes of all of the gargoyles. A welcome to—<u>home?</u> A door opened in the dark tunnel. They went forward slowly. Darkness enveloped her, as she felt small tingles from the spirits. Aiyana followed them trustingly. Somehow, she just knew that it was very safe here.

Finally, there was light ahead. Faint, but there. The light grew. It came from under many doors. One doorway was still dark, and Elan stopped in front of it. She disappeared for a moment.

"This apartment is empty. I just checked," she said to Aiyana.

The door was dark wood, carved with gargoyles and flowers. Brass gleamed in the faint light. Hesitantly, Aiyana put her hand on the ornate lever handle. She pushed it down. The door slowly opened.

Inside was a small condo apartment. Dusty windows went floor to ceiling. Little light made it in, with the dust and some debris outside in its small outer area. She looked for a light switch on the wall, and pushed it. To her amazement, lights came on.

"How?" she asked.

Elan's arm pointed outside. There, in a grassy area, stood a large antique solar panel, gleaming in the sun. The apartment wall held a small Tesla storage battery.

"It all works still!"

"The people here know how to fix old things, I heard," Ava volunteered. Elan nodded confirmation.

The condo was very dirty, though. A thick layer of dust covered everything. Aiyana entered more fully anyway. In the kitchen island, she found a sink. She lifted the faucet lever, and water gushed out, soon going to clean from its rust. Tentatively, she turned on a stove burner. Nothing happened.

Would there be heat in the winter?, she wondered. She had to stay here. Her small amount of hoarded money from her church allowance wouldn't last long. Eventually, she would have to get some sort of job, and perhaps find a newer apartment.

As she pondered, she heard a soft knock on the door, and it opened

slowly and hesitantly.

Chapter 3

Aiyana spun around, fearful of a threat. Could it be the church man, after all? It was – a man? What _was_ he? A ragged hoodie barely concealed an elongated – snout? His face and hands seemed to have fur.

"Don't be afraid. I live next door," he said softly. His voice was slightly growly.

"How? Wh--" Aiyana stuttered out, blushing as she tried to stop staring at the odd sight of him.

"I'm like this because of drugs. Stuck. Like this, in between forms." Dog-like legs propelled him jerkily forward. "I came to welcome you because others are even worse. I'm less of a shock to normal people." A small, sad, doggy type smile accompanied his words. "I'm Kaden. What's your name?"

"Aiyana."

"You speak to the spirits?"

"Yes, and help them to pass to better realms, if they can't on their own."

"Why are you *here*, then? You could be with The ORG."

"The ORG? What is that?" Aiyana asked, puzzled.

"You've never heard of it? They help lots of people. Run soup kitchens, and even leave food here for us."

"Why should I be with them, in particular?" Aiyana was even more puzzled.

"How could you not know?"

"I-- I was at...." Aiyana trailed off. She shouldn't be telling everyone that she met! It wasn't safe to speak of.

"You were at?? Was it that American fanatics church? Them??" Kaden sneered. "Those idiots? We have nothing to do with THEM, obviously!" Kaden motioned to his body. "We have heard whispers of some missing girl of theirs. Even if you ARE that girl, we won't give you up." Kaden looked straight into Aiyana's eyes as he spoke. She could tell that he meant it, and even *felt* his vibration of honesty.

"I am trying to escape from them," Aiyana finally admitted.

"Why come here? Why run from them? They are very rich, and must pay you well. Why are they looking for you? People must leave them sometimes, and have no problems." Kaden's questions came fast.

"I am a very strong spirit talker. Their strongest. But, I do NOT want to be sending any spirit who hadn't joined them to Hell! They will be searching for me. I should leave you in peace. You don't like them, but I could be putting all of you at risk. Ava was supposed to come here, and she suggested it for me. I have her cat/baby. You could take care of her here, without me."

Kaden just looked at her, saying nothing. His mind seemed to be made up about it. Aiyana waited for his response.

"They aren't much here in Canada," he said.

"I know. That's why I came here. To a big city, where I could blend in better...not be noticed...Your area, though, is small..." Aiyana trailed off.

"Toronto is a lot of small neighbourhoods," Kaden smiled. "This one is seen as very rough. Too rough for their more fanatical evangelicals!" He grinned. It was an odd sight, with his slightly hound face, and rather pointy teeth. "The only Arrows here are ones sent here for punishment, for not toeing the line. Like the one out there. He hardly ever says a thing, and gets frightened very easily."

"The spirit guiding me here said that it's the safest place for me, and her child," explained Aiyana. Kaden looked closely at her, and sniffed loudly.

"You smell truthful. You can stay here, until perhaps you find another safe spot. In the ORG, maybe."

"Why are you not sure about The ORG?"

"They keep themselves quiet. Nobody is really sure of what they do. Or, of who they are. Just rumours."

"Oh," Aiyana replied, not quite getting it. He praised The ORG, and then was unsure of it. She then let out a breath of relief. She had somehow lucked out, and was in the most safe place available! "Thank you so much! I'll work hard here, and won't be a burden on anyone!"

"Just helping that little kitten/baby has gotten you in, and is a lot. She belongs here, more than anywhere else," Kaden replied.

The kitten clutched Aiyana with her little hand-paws, and squeaked. Aiyana and Kaden looked at her and smiled.

"It's very safe here," Kaden said. "I'll collect some things from neighbours. Food and other necessities. Some of them work, and bring in money. You will have to get new clothes, though. Yours will give you away fast. Too covered up, loose, and colourless."

"Will I be able to get a job? Anyplace?" Aiyana asked.

"Do you have any office skills, or store related ones?"

"No. I never worked before..." Aiyana trailed off worriedly.

"Well then! First, we need to get you a new identity. Then, we'll see if there are any trainee positions open. I have to get going. I have other work to do in the complex," Kaden said, and left quickly.

"Thanks so much!" Aiyana said to his retreating back. She was lucky to have met someone who knew so much so soon.

*　　　　*　　　　*

"The Arrows are going nuts online! What's up?" Guyan demanded from his elite staff.

"Not sure. They seem to be looking for someone," Jerry answered.

"Why?"

"Some VIP...?" another elite hesitantly answered.

"They would know where all of their VIP's were!" snapped Guyan. "They constantly advertise them, for sure! Find out who it is, and get rid of him! We can't have any of those nuts prowling around in our city and country!" Guyan ordered.

The team quietly dispersed and got to work hacking The Arrows' of God computer systems, to find out exactly what was going on there. Were they looking here at all? Who was missing, and how important was that person? How could the person be missing?

Guyan strode out of the computer hub, to his office area. In reception, a woman dressed in clothes suited to The Arrows of God was standing and crying noisily.

"You <u>have</u> to help me!" she sobbed.

Guyan frowned at the sobbing woman.

"Why come here? You Arrows have your own ghost hunters!" he almost growled. As if they didn't have enough problems with the Arrows!

"My son....he...he...He <u>killed</u> himself! You are the only ones who will help him get to a <u>good</u> afterlife! He was a good boy! Not evil! <u>Not</u> deserving to go to <u>Hell!</u>" She cried into a soggy tissue. Guyan's demeanour softened.

"What was his name, Ma'am?"

"Zachary Miles..." she managed to sniffle out.

"Do you have any photos, and personal items with you?"

"Yes...yes..." she fumbled in her large purse. A ragged paper photo emerged, along with an old style razor.

"OK. We can work with these, and get him over to the Light."

"Thank you! Thank you so <u>much!</u>" The woman grasped Guyan's arm. "Please, don't tell the..the..."

"We do <u>NOT</u> contact <u>them</u> for any reason whatsoever!"

"Thank you!" the woman sobbed out again. Guyan's secretary got up to see to her. "I'll pay anything! Anything at all! Just make sure that my boy is OK!"

"It's OK. It's going to be OK," the secretary soothed as he led the woman out. Guyan shook his head, as he headed back to his team in the computer room.

"Another Arrows of God follower wants our help. Here is a photo of the boy, and his razor. Suicide. His name is Zachary Miles," Guyan told them.

"On it! We will find him, <u>Sir!</u>" Bo made a mock salute, while clicking his heels together.

Guyan frowned at him. "Have I been <u>that</u> bad today, Bo?" Bo grinned at him, but only said, "Let us know if we can help in any way."

"Ohhh—kayyy..." Guyan left the computer and ops room. "What is <u>wrong</u> with me lately?" he wondered to himself. If these bad moods kept up, he'd find himself shifting by accident. That could be a disaster, around vulnerable humans. He shook himself, trying to shake off the feelings of discomfort that had been plaguing him for weeks now. They didn't go away so easily.

Something was in the air. He sensed it. Something big was coming. This unknown possible person from the Arrows might be IT. Or the catalyst for something? He couldn't tell. It bothered him. Usually, his feelings about the future were somewhat clear. This was not.

He went to his desk, to try to crack into the Arrows' systems.

Chapter 4

Aiyana felt herself settling into her new home and surroundings. Just outside of her apartment, she had found a small green space. Once, flowers had grown there. She worked at planting vegetables and more flowers. It would be good to not have to totally rely on the mysterious ORG for food. Meals would be easier for herself and for her new neighbours. Maybe soon to be friends?

"I need a <u>job,</u> though! I need money for things other than just food! And what about winter?" she muttered to herself and the watching kitten.

"ORG office building," a voice said behind her. Aiyana jumped, almost biting her tongue.

"Kaden, you scared me! How can I go there, anyway? I thought that I should <u>avoid</u> The ORG, considering who I am!"

"They have other businesses working there. Outer offices, etc., so that they are concealing themselves a bit."

"How do <u>you</u> know, then?" Aiyana asked, skeptically.

Kaden squatted down, beginning to help her to dig holes. "We have ways of finding out things. Never mind how. You'll figure it out, soon."

"I'm not trained in any office skills!" objected Aiyana.

"Mail and file clerk. Says here that they are hiring in the adjacent building." Kaden held out his arm. It showed a file, showing want ads. He tapped one, and it grew to become readable.

"Trainee needed for mail delivery and filing. No experience necessary. Apply at RoverInc.net/persnl, or in person at 232 Rover Blvd., Basement 212," the ad said.

"Thanks Kaden! Thank you so much!" Aiyana hugged Kaden tightly.

"No problem!" he said in a slightly muffled voice. "Why so happy?"

"I won't have to use the net to apply! I can go there! The Arrows won't find me!"

"You'll still need ID, and a bank for deposits."

"Oh..." Aiyana's face fell.

"Don't worry. We have that covered."

"How? Did you do something already? What?"

"Tonight, "Kaden answered, "I'll take you to our hacker. He'll get legit docs for a new identity for you."

"Legit? Someone's identity will be stolen???" Aiyana was horrified.

"No. Nothing like that! He just does the best fake docs ever! Perfect!"

Aiyana's face lit up again, as her mind filled with hope. Then, a worried frown crossed it, as she thought again. "That must be expensive. I don't have much money left."

"You're planting all of these vegetables for everyone. And, you control ghosts. No violent spirits get in here anymore. We can work out something in barter."

Aiyana closed her eyes, with real relief. Soon, she might be able to support herself entirely. Maybe even get a real apartment, with central heating before winter. Or, at least be better able to contribute here.

That evening, Kaden led her though torturous back alleys and tunnels. Finally, she saw a light shining under a small doorway.

"Duck going in," Kaden quietly told her. He gave a short bark, and the door opened silently. Inside, among candles and dusty piles of books, a large computer screen gleamed. Other, smaller screens surrounded it. Sitting (?) at it, on a strange pedestal sort of thing, was what seemed to be a small bear, or perhaps a very large raccoon. It didn't look at them, so she couldn't see its eyes. It clattered away at a big keyboard.

"Who still uses keyboards?" Aiyana wondered to herself. Forgetting to duck under the doorway, her head bumped a bit on the top. The bear then turned around. Little button eyes, with a black mask around them, glared at them suspiciously. Aiyana, though, felt like smiling. The bearlike creature reminded her of Winnie the Pooh, but with a mask. The bear (or was it raccoon?) glared even more, as if sensing her thoughts.

Kaden swiftly broke through the growing tension. "She needs new I.D., and a history."

The bear turned around to Aiyana, and grated out derisively, with a gravelly voice, "Who are <u>you</u>, then, <u>Human</u>? One of those <u>Arrow</u> idiots, it looks like." He sneeringly looked at her long skirt and long sleeves.

"You can <u>tell</u>? Right away?!" Aiyana squeaked out. This bear was not cuddly at all! Not a bit. Menacing, in fact, in spite of his small size.

"That baggy long dress? That long hair? Of <u>course</u> you are! Nobody else would want to look <u>that</u> awful."

"I—I'll try to change it, once I get a job," said Aiyana nervously.

"CHANGE IT <u>NOW!</u>" the bear shouted. Aiyana backed into Kaden, frightened by the shouting, and the expression of disgust on the bear's face.

"Quit picking on her, Rob! She's <u>hiding</u> from them!"

"Who says?" the sarcastic, derisive tone continued.

"The ghosts and gargoyles say so."

"OK." Suddenly, Rob the bear was businesslike. "New ID, then. What specifically do you need it for?"

"A job? Maybe a new place to live? Some better clothes?" Aiyana answered in a small voice.

"We're not good enough for you here?" sneered Rob.

"You're all wonderful! To help me—I just want to help you, too! I need money. I don't want to be found!"

Rob's eyes went softer. He sniffed, though, before speaking, "Well, since you <u>are</u> hiding from The Arrows, I can help. But first, you have to change up your clothes. You stick out too much as one of <u>them.</u> Probably your hair, too. Mostly, it's your clothes that look odd." He turned back to his computer. "What job are you looking at?"

"I'll send you a link for the ad," answered Kaden. He touched his wrist, and his arm lit up. He poked the link quickly. Rob studied it.

"OK. Good choice there, Kaden. It's been up for a long time. They'll be less picky about details. <u>You,</u>" he turned to Aiyana, "whatever your name is? Forget that name! You'll have a new one. Use it with everyone, not just for work. And...shorten your skirts. Take your tops in! Find someone who sews if you can't do it! You'll look more like a beginner from the burbs or the country. Someplace not as up to the latest styles." Rob turned back to his keyboard. "OK. Any name in mind? Something simple, but not too close to your real name." He handed her a list of names. Aiyana studied it.

"Isi sounds nice," she hesitantly said.

"Good one. Simple, easy to remember. Get everyone that you know to call you Isi from now on. Not your other name at any time. Get used to it, so that you answer to it automatically. Now, I'll pick the last name. Not Smith or Jones. Too often faked, those." Rob scrolled through a list. "Hmmm, let's see what I haven't used yet," he muttered. "Isi Markland. That is your name, from now on!" he continued out loud. "Date of birth, now. How old do you look?" Rob turned around to look at Aiyana/Isi. Young, but not a teen. You want to work full time, and get good wages.

"July 23, 2066, then. You'll be just 19. Old enough to work, drink, and smoke pot. Best to do something, to not seem to be an Arrow in your views." He turned back to the computer, and typed furiously, while Aiyana/Isi thought about drinking and smoking pot. She had been curious for a long time about both.

Suddenly, odd noises erupted from an old looking machine, attached to the computer. Gurgles and whumps and even a hissing noise. Rob hit the black boxy thing with his fist, and papers spewed out of it.

"Have to use the old stuff. Not traceable, and it looks more authentic," Rob explained. He took the papers over to another, very complicated looking machine. It also gurgled and hissed. A laminated card shot across the room, right to where Aiyana/Isi stood. She just managed to catch it.

"Your birth certificate. I put you down as Indigenous. You look it.

Do you know if you are?"

"I'm not sure. I was taken in by The Arrows at a young age. I have a few memories of some things that seem to be Indigenous." She felt puzzled and suddenly unwell, wondering how that could have happened.

"Hmmm," was all that Rob said in reply. Aiyana/Isi looked nervously at him as he typed on. "You have no idea of who your parents were?"

"No."

"We should leave out the Status, anyway. Someone might know who is in the tribe that we put you in," Rob said, after a few more

minutes. "Maybe try braiding your hair, or something," he added.
Aiyana/Isi just stared at him, and wondered about such things. Change
everything about her outer self? Could she do all of that? She decided
to study styles of dress and hair closely.

"How should I dress for the job interview?"

"Conservative, but not dowdy. Just take up your skirt, and take in
your blouse. They should do, for now," Kaden answered her. "Get new
stuff when you get hired."

Aiyana/Isi saw her small savings dwindling, as she got all that was
necessary to just fit in a little. She hoped that the pay was enough for it
all, and that she got this job. She wondered about a tattoo. One would
definitely set her apart from The Arrows.

"All done!" Rob said, gathering up a bunch of papers. "Study these
closely. These are your imagined school marks, and schools, plus other
things about the new you. Decide if you went to the Prom, and what
you wore. Women like to know that stuff. It wouldn't have been long
ago, so you might get asked about it. Now, get lost! I hope that I won't
have to see you again! That would mean that you slipped up." Rob
growled.

Kaden took "Isi's" (she had to think of herself as that!) arm, and
propelled her out quickly.

"Wow! He liked you!" Kaden exclaimed.

"???" Isi stared at him.

"Usually, Rob hardly says a word! And, he never gives out advice!
You're so lucky! He knows all about these things. Better than anyone
else living here. Good for you, Isi!" Kaden grinned at her.

"Thanks for letting me know...I guess," Aiyana/Isi replied. "When
should I apply for the job?"

Kaden looked at his arm again, and poked it twice. "Wow!" he
exclaimed. "Rob sent in the application for you!" He looked in awe at

Aiyana/Isi. "Interview Monday at 8:30 a.m. So fast! He must have made you look good, to get one so soon!"

Aiyana/Isi—she <u>had</u> to think of herself as Isi!--felt flustered, though. "But, I have so much to do! Only today and the weekend to study who I am now, and to get some clothes altered. And, to fix my hair, too! My hair!"

"What about your hair?"

"I don't want to cut it! Even if I did have the money for it!"

Kaden looked at her, considering. "You could do a braid. Rob suggested that," he said.

"I need to ask another girl. Maybe Elen will help me," Isi said to herself, then she called out with her mind, "Elen! Elen!"

Elen's cheerful, ghostly presence came right away. Her essence surrounded Isi.

"What is it, Aiyana?" she asked.

"Call me 'Isi' now. It's my new name," Isi explained from her mind. "I have to get used to it."

"Ah- I see. Rob was good to you, then?"

"Kaden says that Rob likes me!" Isi said aloud, so that Kaden could hear.

"Rob also needs help," Elen said softly.

"Are you talking to a ghost now?!" Kaden asked. His eyes were a bit wide and frightened.

"Half a wolf/dog, and you are afraid of <u>ghosts??</u>" Isi teased.

"Well...ummmm...." Kaden stammered.

"Anyway, I need help with my hair and clothes for this job," Isi explained to Elen, glad to not go into Rob's problems. She had no idea of how to help him. "So...Now, to <u>work!</u>"

"Work?" Kaden and Elen both asked.

"Clothes!" They all laughed, and went off together.

For a few days, Isi/Aiyana stitched frantically, under the advice of Elen, and other female spirits. She hemmed shorter skirts, and tightened blouses and dresses.

"What about my <u>hair?</u> " she kept asking Elen. She held it up, long, straight, and black. Right to her waist. Too likely to be noticed by The Arrows, perhaps. Finally, Elen looked at her closely.

"Maybe cut some bangs, and colour parts of it? Can you afford some temporary colours? Spray on ones?"

"No, not really."

"Anyone have any ideas?" Elen asked the group of women spirits surrounding Isi. Most looked blank.

"Hmmm!--I know!" Ava suddenly exclaimed. "Plants! Boil some flowers, or leaves! I sometimes did that, when out of money. I'll point out which ones work best on dark hair."

The work continued. Isi had a few skirts above her knees now; what she thought were sexy tops, and a few streaks of reddish colour in her black hair. She finally felt ready for her interview. She was puzzled by how long it had been posted. Apparently, it had been up for months!

"Most people these days are over qualified for that sort of job,"

Kaden explained.

The day arrived.

"How do I look?" Isi asked Elen and Kaden. She had added blue streaks to the red ones that morning. Her straight skirt was just above her knees, and her blouse felt just a little too tight for her comfort.

"Your hair looks good. But—you <u>will</u> need more stylish clothes soon," Kaden pronounced. "This outfit is perfect for the job interview. Not too stylish, but also not dowdy." Isi breathed a sigh of relief, and prepared herself for going out for the first time in months.

As she passed the gargoyles, green eyes flashed with lights. Then, she was out alone in the city. She passed the pimp, who studiously ignored her. Then, The Arrow converter agent, who looked at her with disgust, as if she was an Evil Slut. Isi—she had to think of herself as only Isi—felt like giggling about his pursed lip glare. She grinned at him, instead. His eyes bugged out, as he glared even more. Happiness and relief filled Isi. He no longer could see her as perhaps one of <u>theirs.</u> She happily walked to the subway, while checking her palm sized map for directions to the interview building.

Getting off, the contrast was extreme. Clean streets; sparkling, intact glass in all of the buildings. Flowers and trees were almost covering the sidewalks. The one that she wanted was one of several buildings connected by 'vator tubes. She could tell that the windows were all solar windows.   Robot taxis lined the street in front of them. A wide double door was in the main building. Isi checked the number, and the arrow point on her map.

Gulping slightly, she went to the doors. They opened up majestically before her. Nervously, she passed into the massive foyer. Trees, a living wall of flowers, and a gurgling fountain met her. An urge came over Isi to run back out the doors. She had passed a small forested area on the way here. Maybe she could hide there for a bit, and catch her breath? Shaking off her strange mood, Isi searched around the plants, to see if there was a reception desk somewhere in this indoor forest of The ORG.

Chapter 5

As she searched, Isi then began to wonder if she should just go home. Back to The Arrows. At least they were familiar. The ORG? She was supposed to <u>avoid</u> it, but also be employed by it?? It was very confusing and upsetting. No. Just NO. She would not go back to The Arrows. She had escaped their clutches, and was finally free. No more being forced to believe their awful religion and ways of life. She had made it here. People here liked her, and weren't just using her for her strange talent.

Isi kept on going, and finally saw the reception desk. It was covered in flower pots. Of course. She went up to a friendly looking guard.

"I'm here for an interview for the mailroom?"

"Great! I'll just buzz for a guide," he said, looking slightly surprised. He pressed a button, and a small robot rolled across the shiny bamboo floor.

"May we help you?" it asked.

"She's here for the mailroom job," the guard answered.

"Vator C, to Level 102, section 3," the metallic voice said. "Follow." It rolled off, and Isi hurried to catch up, calling out a thanks to the friendly guard. She felt slightly dazed. She had never been in a place so automated.

"C" vators were the ones that went between buildings, the sign at the vator said. Isi joined several people in the vator that the robot stopped in front of.

"Hi! Where to?" a friendly man asked.

"102, Section 3, I was told," Isi answered.

"Oh! Mail Recruitment! You must be applying, then. I'm nearby, and will help you find it. Don't worry." He smiled kindly at her. Isi hesitantly smiled back, then she felt her stomach drop when the vator went up with a whoosh. Her stomach was still down someplace...maybe the basement...when the vator paused, and then zoomed sideways.

"Oh!" a soft cry of surprise came out of her, as her eyes widened.

"You'll get used to it," the kind man said. "In a few weeks, it'll be nothing!"

"You think that I'll get the job?"

"For sure! Hardly anyone wants to be at the bottom anymore. Not with all of their training."

Isi must have looked alarmed, because her new acquaintance said reassuringly, "Don't worry. Kitzi is a lovely person. Nicest girl that you'll ever meet! Our stop is coming up soon!" he continued, as people got off at many places. They were soon the only ones left on the vator.

Finally, it came to a smooth stop, and the man led Isi into another area that was filled with plants and flowers. A waterfall went down one wall, and filled a pond with water lilies. Light tubes let in concentrated sunlight. No artificial lights were on, on this sunny day. The air smelled of flowers and greenness.

"This way!" the friendly man said. "By the way, my name's Jerry. what's yours?"

"Ai—ai—Isi, Jerry" Isi stumbled over her new name.

"Ai-isi?"

"N-no. Just Isi," she replied nervously.

"OK." Jerry looked at her with a question in his eyes, but said nothing, fortunately. He just took her across the main area to a large and colourful metal door. At his knock, it slid into the walls silently.

"Hey Kitzi! You finally have an applicant! Here is—Isi!" He bowed and swept his hands as if doing a magic act.

"Jerry! Are you joking again?"

"Nope!" Jerry stood aside, to reveal Isi.

"Oh my!" The woman who came up to them was rather startlingly dressed. She was the most colourfully dressed person that Isi had ever seen. Her long blonde hair had pink, blue, and purple streaks. Her very short pink dress seemed to have flashing coloured lights somewhere under it. She wore pink and blue paisley leggings. Her shoes, though, were the most odd of all. They were a deeper pink, with tall heels that flashed lights on and off. Those lights at times sparkled on down to her toes.

"New shoes, I see! Wonderful effects!" Jerry complimented Kitzi. Kitzi grinned, as she looked down happily at her shoes.

"Thanks Jerr! And thanks so much for bringing Isi here. I'll see you at break, then?"

"For sure, Kitzi! Bye now! Have to rush!" Jerry replied as he turned to go.

"Thank you so much, again..." Isi began, but Jerry had already rushed through the door. She turned and smiled nervously at Kitzi. Kitzi smiled warmly at her.

"Do you have an application with you?" Kitzi asked. "I saw yours online, but I may need more information."

"N-no," Isi felt even more nervous. What more information could she provide? "No printer at home. Sorry!"

"No difference. Here, finish up some of the spaces on the computer here. It's logged in already."

Isi got to work, trying to be discreet about checking her notes about her assumed history. In the background, Kitzi sorted packages and boxes that had arrived at the office. When Isi had finished the form, she turned around. Kitzi noticed, and came over to her. She quickly read over the application.

"OK. Decent grades. No employment history, but you are quite young. No college or other courses taken after high school?"

"N-no. I'm sorry..." I really need to stop stammering, Isi told herself. She must look very suspicious. Kitzi didn't seem to notice, or care, though.

"OK! Not a problem! In fact, it's probably even better for me! You won't be looking for a better job after a week or two. And, most importantly, you won't be telling me how to do my job!" Kitzi laughed. "Well, let's have you do some tests, then," she continued. "Just for alphabetizing, and general sorting. This is a big place. You need to be able to sort for different departments, and even companies, as well."

Isi's nerves began to settle, as Kitzi's warm and welcoming manner washed over her. Kitzi might be oddly dressed, but she seemed to be very nice.

"Plus," Isi thought to herself, "I'm happy that no <u>way</u> would Kitzi go over well with The Arrows of God!" She smiled for the first time that day. Kitzi smiled warmly back at her.

*   *   *

Guyan was looking over his online reports, when a ping came through from his secretary. He pushed a button to hear what the news was.

"The mailroom job seems to have finally been filled," his secretary reported.

"Someone actually <u>wanted</u> that job? Who? When?"

"There's not much on record about her. Just basic school stuff. But, she almost dresses like those Arrows of God twits."

"If they sent someone here, they may have heard of our work," Guyan pondered for a moment. "And, will want to stop it, if it's confirmed. Keep an ear out, and an eye, as well," he ordered.

"Will do," the secretary answered. "I'll see if anyone can be spared."

"Do that. I'll try to meet her casually; get an impression and a sniff," Guyan decided. "What did you mean by, 'Sort of dresses like an Arrow?'"

"She seems to have some sort of hair dye, and shorter skirts."

"Hmm. Who reported on this?" Guyan asked.

"Jerry Tate, in graphic designs."

"He <u>does</u> know his fashion, so he would know best about her style," Guyan grinned.

"He certainly knows fashion! Jerry vouches for her being "nice" and "sweet", though, too."

"Jerry is a good judge of character," Guyan admitted. "I will still go and check her out myself. Jerry can keep an eye on her in general, though."

Guyan sat, thinking of the recent reports of an unknown source of upset in the Arrows' offices. Then, this strange girl shows up <u>here</u>? So conveniently?

"Both at once? Unlikely to be any coincidence," he said to himself.

"Zolie, find me something to do with the mailroom. Have a fake parcel delivery," he ordered.

"Yes, <u>Sir!</u>"

Guyan rolled his eyes. Secretaries. Thought that they ran everything.

"Whenever you can," he said sarcastically. A chuckle came over the

com, and it clicked off.

*   *   *

In the mailroom, Isi had finished the tests, and waited anxiously for Kitzi to let her know the results. She thought that she had done well, but it still was hard to wait.

"A perfect score!" Kitzi announced with a huge smile. "Welcome to the ORG, Isi! When can you start?"

Isi felt slightly stunned. She had done perfectly?! And that was it? No more tests or interviews? If she wanted to, she could start right now. She hoped to—money was tight.

"I could start right now..." she began, hesitantly.

"Great!" Kitzi exclaimed happily. "I'm sure that we'll get along wonderfully! And, that you'll learn fast, with perfect scores!"

Isi blinked. Kitzi beaming was quite a sight. Kitzi's whole face lit up with delight. And this was just over hiring someone? Isi smiled back. Kitzi was so much herself that Isi also smiled easily around her, in spite of her worries about working for the mysterious and possibly dangerous ORG.

"This is so great!" Kitzi went on. "I'll bring you down to the basement mail area, for our morning parcels. You will be in charge of parcels. We get deliveries twice a day." Kitzi then swept out of the door, holding it for Isi to follow. They headed for another set of vators. These were labelled "Utility".

"Now," Kitzi seemed to put on a 'lecturing' face, Isi thought. "Some people say that there are ghosts down there, and won't go near the place! Do ghosts frighten you at all, Isi?"

"N-no, not really..." Isi had no idea of what to say, or how to say it.

"Great! That is, if you truly aren't frightened?" Kitzi looked searchingly at her. Isi smiled reassuringly. Kitzi smiled widely. "They've never hurt anyone, if they are really there. I don't see why people get so scared." They got onto the large vator, and it shot down to the bowels of the building.

Isi hoped that the ghosts weren't pushy ones. She didn't want to be seen speaking to them, and look either crazy or suspicious. She just wanted to properly learn the job, and do well at it. She liked it here.

The whole complex had a fresh, clean and welcoming feel to it; and Kitzi was a warm and happy sort of person. Kitzi began to explain her duties, and some of the procedures. Isi pulled herself from a nice daydream of working here quietly until retirement.

    The Parcel Room was bright and colourful. Bold, abstract patterns filled the walls, and each desk was a different colour. Isi blinked at what should have been a mishmash, but somehow it all worked together.

    "Do you like it?" Kitzi eagerly asked. "I'm the one who did it all!" She smiled, a bit nervously.

    "It's wonderful!" answered Isi. "Like a flower garden, somehow! I thought that it would be all grey in here!"

    "It was! I couldn't <u>stand</u> it! Do you—ummm---like the glittery bits?"

    "They are just <u>perfect</u>!" Isi avowed. Kitzi's smile turned radiant.

    "I'm so glad that you like it! I thought that I'd be the only one to see it, so it didn't matter what I did. But now, <u>you</u> are here! And you like it, <u>too</u>!"

    "You are a real artist, Kitzi!" Isi thought that Kitzi might hug her, she was so overjoyed. They smiled at each other.

    As they went through the parcels, Isi felt tingling on her neck. 'It must be a ghost," she thought to herself, so ignored it. Then, she heard the vator doors swoosh. The tingling increased. Why would a ghost use a vator? As their door opened, Kitzi looked up from her explanations on how to tag each parcel, for their robots to deliver.

    "Oh, Mr. Orzon! My goodness! Can we help you? Are you looking for a parcel?"

"No," Guyan said shortly, as he looked around the colourful room with surprise. Isi turned around, to see who had touched her Awareness.

In front of her stood a well built Indigenous man, with hard, rather suspicious looking eyes. His black hair was swept back into a long braided pony tail. He was tall and commanding, with strikingly handsome features. Isi shivered, not sure if it was from fear, or something else. She felt him too much. She had never felt this tingling Awareness before. Not from anyone living, and not so strongly, even from spirits. The two stood and stared at each other.

"This is my new helper, Isi Markland," Kitzi said, looking slightly nervous about the tension. "Isi, this is Mr. Orzon, the head of The ORG." Her eyes darted back and forth between them.

Isi's eyes widened. The man in front of her radiated power of more than the money-making kind. She almost felt that she should curtsy to him! He looked back at her, with even more suspicion.

He saw a young, small, but rather curvy Indigenous woman, with long black hair, that was streaked with blue and red. Her clothes did little for her, being rather shapeless, but at least her skirt was short enough to show lovely legs. It was only a bit above the knee, much to his disappointment. Guyan caught himself. He was supposed to be checking out her motives, not her body! He tried a slight probe, but got nothing. A natural block? He then subtly sniffed, but could only smell probably natural nerves at meeting The Boss so soon. Kitzi was actually more nervous.

Isi kept her mental shields tight, feeling his probe. She made her thoughts go boringly "normal", just in case. If he did get through, he might get too bored to really try a deeper probe. Guyan did sense her very bland thoughts, and he felt even more suspicious. He began to push out a deeper probe, but stopped himself. What was he thinking? It was very wrong to probe at all, based on just a vague suspicion, and here he was, going for a deep probe?

Sure, she did dress somewhat like The Arrows, with only a shorter skirt. That proved nothing about her beliefs. No reason for her to be denied a job. And, she seemed to be accepting of the extreme fashions of Kitzi. Also, had been easily friendly to Jerry, who also had rather wild fashions. Guyan pulled himself together.

"Nice to meet you, Ms Markland." He held out his hand.

Isi's hand was slim and small in his big warm hand. A shock went through her, and she said something in reply. She wasn't sure what it was. Nobody looked at her oddly, so she assumed that it was appropriate. Who was this man, really? What powers did he have? Something radiated from him.

Guyan felt a shock of his own as his hand engulfed Isi's. He looked down into her deep black eyes for an instant, seeing similar shock in her eyes. What was wrong with him? What power over him did this small and feminine woman have?

Both of them stepped back quickly. Too quickly. Kitzi looked at them with puzzlement. Then, seeing their expressions as they refused to look at each other, her eyes cleared, and she smiled widely.

"I'm having a party to celebrate getting my folding robot next month! Both of you are invited!" Kitzi exclaimed.

Two pairs of black eyes turned to stare at her. Where did that idea come from so suddenly? Kitzi smirked. If she couldn't tell when two people were attracted to each other, then who could? And these two were so obvious about it, that anyone could! Not that she was doing so well in the romance department. She could see it so well in everyone else, but she seemed to be always confused about her own love life. But, next weekend, The Night would change all of her boyfriend's coldness towards her!Kitzi's eyes shone about her vision of happiness, and also about her unwitting victims. They had no clue!

Isi felt overwhelmed. She had wanted to keep a low profile. She was told to do so around The ORG, especially. Yet, here she was, invited to a party, where the Boss, the head of The ORG, was also invited? She politely smiled her acceptance, though.

Guyan's smile looked slightly feral, with a haughty, cat-like expression. He should certainly keep his eye on this young woman.

(Not that he'd have any trouble looking at her, something in him said.) Some sort of power was in her, but he couldn't quite pick up what it might be. He stared assessingly at her. Isi felt worried and confused. Why did The Boss keep on staring at her so suspiciously? Would she now lose this wonderful job, and potential new friend?

Guyan said nothing to that effect, though. Only saying, "Good choice for your new hire, Kitzi," he left, as abruptly as he had arrived.

"Well! I wonder what he wanted down here? Very odd for anyone to to visit here, let alone <u>Mr. Orzon</u>!" Kitzi puzzled. "Oh well! No use speculating about bosses! They just love to see people working for them, and <u>that</u> we <u>were</u> doing! Back to work!

"Isi, you load most of the parcels onto the robots, and then log where they are going, <u>here</u>" Kitzi showed her the screens. "Now, there are often parcels that need to be hand-delivered. Mr. Orzon usually gets those types, and others on his floors, too. For Mr. Orzon, you use this special vator—it only goes to his floor." Kitzi pointed to a second, smaller vator doorway. "I'll register your fingerprint so that you can go there, and give you a list of everyone else on those floors. So, let's do a trial run of the parcels that are here."

Isi carefully scanned packages, and put them into the robot carriers.

"Now, you see that the robots can pick up larger boxes on their own. Push this icon for large boxes," Kitzi continued. The selected robot whirred into action, and picked up a huge box on its under lift. Slowly, Isi scanned more boxes and parcels, and she and Kitzi put them on top of the biggest boxes, or into the carrier. Whirring quietly, the robot then smoothly rolled to the vator. A claw-like appendage shot out of it, and it punched the vator button.

"See! Nothing more to do! You put in the proper codes, and the robots know exactly which floor to go to, and even the right locations on each floor." Kitzi was looking at the computer manifest as she spoke. "You did so well for the first time! Everything is right for that robot! Let's do a few more together while I'm here, and then I can leave you to yourself down here. I'll be monitoring you on the computer, and will let you know if you've made a mistake. Are you sure that you're not afraid of any potential ghosts?"

"Oh no! Not at all!" Isi said, looking up from the scanner.

"Great! I was worried about getting another 'Sensitive'! They always get scared off!"

Isi smiled with relief. She still had the job, and no one here seemed to have any idea that she had any abilities at all. She'd not see Mr. Orzon again, most likely. Not until Kitzi's party, and he should be easy to avoid in a crowd. She would wait until she was alone to speak to whoever was down here, and see if they wanted to stay or go on to the next life.

Chapter 6

Several days passed, as Isi settled into her new routine. The kitten usually woke her up, by walking around her head and patting her face. She would dress in her newly styled clothes, and head off to the subway. Everything was calm. Isi began to relax more and more.

The spirits who preferred to stay in the basement had become friends. She never felt alone or lonely while working. Whenever she saw Kitzi, Kitzi congratulated her on how well she was doing. Kitzi was a good and friendly boss, and Isi was happy with her job. It was always the same, but the spirits often entertained her with their antics. Some would do the typical haunting "Woooo's", to make her laugh. Doors would open and close. Some just talked to her about their former lives.

She had not had to see the alarming Mr. Orzon again. (Such a relief!) Maybe he was like that to all new employees? She tried hard to not think about him, but kept on thinking of his looks, anyway. Of all of the people that she could be attracted to, it had to be not just her boss, but also someone who didn't seem to trust her? Kitzi sometimes sighed, which made the spirits get alarmed.

But then, one day, there was a package for him.

She looked at it as if it might bite. Which, having met Mr. Orzon, it possibly would do! She kept on turning the small box in her hands, hoping that it would change its direction and person. It didn't oblige. The package seemed to radiate suspicion and psychic power. No spirits were attached to it, so she couldn't ask it about its reasons for being there. She would just have to deliver it, unfortunately. She hoped that Mr. Orzon wouldn't be there, or that he had a secretary to take his parcels. She did not want to see him again!

Kitzi's party loomed ahead, of course. Where she would have to play hide and seek with the overwhelmingly handsome man. It didn't help that she felt so attracted to him.

"Usually, the secretary takes parcels, I'm sure," Isi told herself. She relaxed. She would not have to be close to that man again. She could avoid him easily at the party. He would not be seeking out a Nobody, who was in his company's lowest job, after all. She convinced herself that she had just imagined his eyes being so searching and suspicious when looking at her. He probably had just been wondering about anyone who took this job. It had been open for a very long time, after all. She had just been worried about keeping the job, so made a big deal out of very little, Isi kept telling herself.

Now that she was established here, and he had not said anything against her, she could stop worrying about getting fired. He had probably mostly forgotten about her, after all. Kitzi was the one to decide to keep her on or not.

Guyan watched the camera feeds from the parcel room. He hadn't seen Isi do anything unusual or strange in the past few weeks, but somehow, he just could not stop watching her. The graceful way that she moved; the ways that she'd flip her long black hair back, or tuck it behind her ears. All of it fascinated him.

He swore at himself. Odd things about her were what he should be looking for—not things that made him get hard. Uncomfortably, he adjusted his position behind his desk. He growled, as he even felt his teeth and claws start to extend. He made himself turn from the enticing camera, to look at current financial statements. Those should calm his raging libido!

Lately, Isi had been feeling as if she was being watched. No new spirits had come out to speak to her, though. The feeling of eyes on her stopped suddenly. She relaxed. Had she been imagining things? Then, she saw the spirits, as they materialized.

"You are being watched," said a deep spirit voice. It was an Ancient Indigenous man speaking. Wisdom shone in his eyes.

"What are you doing here, in this place?" Isi felt puzzled, as she thought at the spirit. "Was it a burial ground?" She felt anger rise in her at the thought.

"I fell here in battle," was the reply. Relief filled Isi. She would not have known what to do if it had been a burial ground.

"Do you need help to pass on to the next phase?" she politely asked him.

"No, I can easily come and go. I find this place—interesting."

"I see. Do you know of any spirits here who do need help crossing over?"

"I help them," the stern warrior said. Isi felt relieved. The watcher, whoever it was, would not see her sending spirits on here.

"Thank you for your visit and information, warrior. I am honoured by your visit to me," she said to him.

"The watcher will not hurt or harm you," the spirit suddenly said. He then vanished into the light. Isi went back to work, feeling a lot less worried about being caught here, at The ORG. She mostly worked in this room, after all. She hoped to not encounter any spirits in other areas. Kitzi had not spoken of any ghostly activity anywhere else.

Still—she did have that package to hand deliver to Mr. Orzon's office. She squared her shoulders, and picked up The Ominous Box, then headed for his private vator.

Chapter 7

"Mr. Orzon!" the voice came into his office, as Guyan studied reports on his computer.

"What?" Guyan growled. Even financial statements and predictions couldn't keep his head away from the temptations of Isi.

"The Arrows are spreading out all over the city! We've even found some of those so-called 'Recruiters' here! Right in front of The ORG towers!"

"Are they as pushy as usual?"

"Yep! For sure!"

"Let those ones be. It's illegal to be pushy, so probably they put the dumber ones around us. We <u>don't</u> want any smart ones here!"

"Are they looking for something? Do you know what it is"

"Or who..." Guyan muttered.

"Mr. O.? What did you say?"

"Doesn't matter. They won't find a thing on our turf. Just keep an eye on them."

"Will do!" Both of them signed off. Guyan then wondered if he should have a chat with the delectable—wait! <u>WHAT</u>? Delectable? What the...____...his brain kept on going there! He forced the word away. He wondered if he should have a chat with the <u>real</u> Isi Markland. Or whatever her name really was. He drummed what he suddenly realized were claws on his desk, so forced them back into his fingers. How to get her to speak for <u>real</u>?

Isi had seen all of the Arrow recruiters. They were building up everywhere. She knew that they were looking for her. Better camouflage was now very necessary. Her first pay had come in. Could she afford new clothes with it? What were the prices like here? Where to find clothes totally unlike her Arrow clothes? The dumbest recruiters might notice her, if she kept to just her remade Arrow wardrobe. She needed bright, trendy, and short new clothes. Also, to get to them without being spotted by the recruiters who seemed to surround The ORG buildings. She thought hard.

Well, she had put off The Package for way too long now. She geared herself up, and took to the vator. At a large desk, a secretary took it, and her angst was over with. All of that for nothing! Returning to her basement, she pondered again about her clothing. Suddenly, it came to her to just ask Kitzi. She hit the button to speak to her.

"Is there a way to the subway and shopping, without going outside?" Isi tentatively asked Kitzi.

"Of course! The shopping concourse goes all over downtown! You'll love going places that way! Do you want to do some shopping, then?" Kitzi was excited for Isi. She had several ideas for updating Isi's look. "I can tell you the best places to buy new clothes! With great deals, too!" Kitzi grinned about the idea of going shopping.

Isi thought for a moment. If she went with Kitzi, the recruiters would mostly notice Kitzi, with her wildly colourful outfits and hair. Having help finding the best stores would also be good, along with Kitzi's advice on fashion. Anything that Kitzi chose would definitely not look like Arrow clothes!

Grinning back at Kitzi, she said, "I'd love to have your help! It will be so much fun!"

"I know!" exclaimed Kitzi. "I can't wait to show you some of my favourite stores! They're all very wonderful! I'll see you after work!" They smiled at each other as they clicked off, to get back to work.

At the end of the day, Isi found herself about to go shopping with her friendly supervisor. Turquoise doors with a mural on them, led out from the basement into a new world of stores, lights, and smells of foods. Light tubes opened to the streets above and let in natural daylight. Crowds hurried by, on their ways to other buildings or shopping.

"Come with me!" Kitzi dashed off so quickly to the right, that Isi had to run to catch up with her. And—there was a store! Filled with amazingly coloured clothes. Isi followed Kitzi into the store, feeling slightly stunned. The clothes weren't just colourful, but some seemed to move on their own, while others had twinkling lights. All of the skirts were very short. Isi gulped. Could she wear anything that short? She noticed a recruiter outside the store, looking at her. She bolstered her mind about short skirts. She could not be noticed by even junior Arrows!

"This red will really suit you, Isi!" Kitzi called out from the depths of a rack of dresses. It was a deep, burgundy red. The hem went up and down, so that not all of it was extremely short. A burgundy that was almost black trimmed its collar and short sleeves. Isi fell in love at first sight. It was so wonderful!

"Let's get you sized!" Kitzi pushed a nearby button, and a saleswoman who seemed to be wearing nothing but pulsing lights came up to them.

"Isi here needs new clothes!" Kitzi gestured to Isi. The saleswoman's extreme head dress swayed as she nodded. Overly blue eyes looked at Isi.

"Do we have your sizes in our data base?" she asked her.

"No," Isi softly said, looking down. She was afraid to stare at the oddly dressed woman. Was this a usual sort of outfit? She hoped not!

"Well, then, come with me!" They followed the large swaying head

dress to the back of the store.

A pretty robot girl waited at the sizing rooms. Cameras in her dark eyes recorded their approach. Isi could see two rooms. The outer room said, "Clothes Room". At Kitzi's gesture to go, Isi went into that room. The robot girl followed her in.

"Give me your garments," the robot said, in a soft, light voice. 'She' held 'her' arms out. "Then go through the second door, and stand in the centre 'X'."

Isi placed her clothes carefully onto the out-stretched, human-like arms of the robot. She then saw that it had rollers under its long dress. She stepped into the circular second room, and onto the large white 'X' in its centre. The door automatically closed, and various coloured lights streamed over heer whole body, while soothing music played.

"Measuring is done," a musical female voice said, and the door opened again. Isi quickly dressed, as the robot stood still, looking rather like an old style mannequin. Having never seen a humanoid robot before, Isi felt slight awkward, in spite of its immobility.

"Th-thank you," she stammered out, feeling that she should say something to it...(her?)

"You are very welcome!" Only the robot's face moved when it spoke. It was very eerie. Isi was glad to leave the measuring rooms.

"Isn't it _fun_, getting measured?!" Kitzi bubbled.

Isi just nodded. "It certainly is interesting."

On a rack outside the changing rooms, the new burgundy dress in her size was already hanging.

"I told the salesgirl which one you wanted, and she punched it in while you were being measured!" Kitzi told her. "They are _so_ good in this store! I can hardly wait to see it on you! Go and try it on!"

"Oh yes! Maybe I'll wear it right now," answered Isi. She _had_ to shake off the suspicious recruiter right away!

"You are _just_ like me!" Kitzi's turquoise eyes sparkled. "I can't _wait_ to wear my new clothes, too! What about new shoes, then, too?" She went rushing off to find matching shoes.

Isi left the store in her new dress and shoes. The dress swirled around her, giving just glimpses of her upper legs. The black and burgundy shoes, with small heels, were a bit hard to walk in. In a pink glittery bag, she carried a glittery long dress, that had translucent panels on its sides. Kitzi had proclaimed that Isi's legs were so good, that she _had_ to show them off.

Isi felt pretty and provocative. A certain suspicious man should now look at her differently! She shook herself, before going too far into a daydream about black eyes and good shoulders... 'He' was off limits, for too many reasons to count.

Outside the store, the recruiter was still there, with his bundles of pamphlets. He gave both women disgusted looks, and turned away. Isi was now a Fallen Woman, by showing off her body. In the eyes of the Arrows, she was now bound for Hell. She smiled.

"Isn't it great?" Kitzi exclaimed. Isi grinned back at her. "I'll have to go shopping with you a lot! It's really fun! Oh look! There's Jerry! Jerry! JERRY!" Kitzi called out. Jerry turned and smiled.

"Kitzi! Hi! And Isi, too! Isi, you look wonderful! That colour suits you. You look so beautiful in it!"

"Are you shopping, too?" Kitzi asked him.

"Oh yes!" replied Jerry. "I just bought these new shoes. The lights are like those old neon ones that they used to use. See?" Jerry held his foot out. Dark purple lights in tubes swirled around his shiny black shoes. Isi blinked, slightly stunned, as he held up his foot for inspection. Jerry grinned at Isi's reaction.

"Don't worry," he teasingly said. "You can find some just like these! They're in women's styles, too!" Isi grinned back at him. Kitzi surprisingly paid little attention to Jerry's shoes. She was looking around.

"Ummmm...Jerry, have you seen Ralphie around recently?" she asked, with a too casual look on her face.

"Are you still seeing that awful poet, Kitzi?" he demanded.

"But---he's a poet! He's so Deep!" Kitzi argued. Jerry rolled his eyes. Isi wondered why, but said nothing.

"I so want you to meet him, too, Isi!" gushed Kitzi. "You are so quiet and deep, too, that I'm sure that you will understand his Great Poetry! He wants to be just like Nik Beat, you know!"

"Oh," was all that Isi could think of saying. She had not been allowed to read any of Nik Beat's poetry, but had managed to sneak a peak when at a book store now and then. She wondered if Ralphie was trying to copy him, or just be famous like Nik Beat.

Across the mall, another Arrow recruiter eyes suddenly grew hard and angry. He stared at the small, happy group, then muttered a few words; apparently to himself. The embedded pick-up in his jawbone caught his words.

"Checking a subject," he said.

"Visuals?" a voice answered. The recruiter blinked twice rapidly, turning his eyes to the group. Cameras in his contacts clicked.

Isi, Kitzi, and Jerry were joking about themselves doing poetry, while laughing a lot about silly rhyming words. Jerry's monitors picked up a faint signal. He glanced casually at the recruiter, and saw the glassiness of special contacts. He glanced away again, and gave another silly word to the rhymes. Isi and Kitzi both laughed. Jerry kept the recruiter in his peripheral vision, while he joked with them.

The remote viewer looked closely at the group. At Isi in her new outfit, parti-coloured hair and all. At Kitzi, with her very short skirt, and sparkling over the knee boots. At Jerry, subtly overdressed, but extremely stylish.

"That group? Of sleazes?" the viewer sneered.

"The Native girl does have long black hair, and--" the recruiter began.

"Don't waste our time!" the viewer snapped. He cut the connection with an audible click.

The recruiter kept on staring, though. He wondered, should he follow them, or not? He so wanted to advance past this frustrating "Recruiter" status. It was boring, and he only got dirty looks all day. No new recruits here!

Jerry took note of how the sharp-eyed man kept watching them; memorizing his looks, and how he moved. He pretended to fiddle with his tie, as he took a quick photo. The recruiter then got a hit, and had to start a spiel to some poor victim. The shopper looked harassed and tired, and seemed to just be trying to be polite.

Kitzi looked enquiringly at Jerry. "What's over there?"

"A recruiter for The Arrows. Too many of them lately!" Jerry replied angrily. He noted Isi going suddenly stiff, a look of fear in her eyes.

"They're all so stupid!" Kitzi proclaimed. "Anyone around The ORG would be taken in for harassment, or moved on!"

"Yes, that poor woman now looks very glassy eyed, with the spiel at her!" Jerry joked.

He took both women by their arms, saying, "Let's do more shopping! Isi needs more than one work outfit! And, I have heard of some video ties! I need to get one of those!" Isi grinned, and they drifted out of the orbit of the strangely nosy Arrow recruiter.

The recruiter shrugged, as he continued on with his spiel to the glassy-eyed woman. No way would such an important person in The Arrows be wearing such a revealing outfit, he thought. Nor be seen with those two. She had looked too comfortable and happy with them, to be any Arrow girl.

The trio strolled on, and into a large men's store. There were several exits, on different levels, Jerry knew. Isi looked around her. More colourful clothes. She smiled at her friends.

Done with his spiel, the recruiter handed many pamphlets to the bored and reluctant woman. He then clicked his tongue, to connect again.

"Can you follow them?"

"Look—we are not going to waste manpower and resources to follow stupid sleazes who happen to have long black hair, and look 'Indian'! Don't you know how many Indians are in that stupid city??" the connection snapped shut.

The recruiter had a sudden urge to dig his connector out of his bones, and run away like that 'Agatha' (or whatever her name was) had done. He wondered how she had managed to not just escape the main compound, but also get rid of her tracking device, and then get across the border, all without being noticed. And then, to disappear completely. Did they even know which country she had gone to? Did they have people looking in Mexico? Had anyone looked at airports?

He wished that he could do the same. He was so very tired of all of the silly rules, and being looked down on by everyone. He gave up a good paying, if boring job, for that? He wanted to follow her, to ask her how she had done it. But then, they would find her, and neither of them would be free. He wished her all the best, and let go of his gut feelings on her. She sure had looked great in that sexy red dress.

Chapter 8

There was another Package for Mr. Orzon. She had put off delivering it for most of the day. It was time. The first one had been so easy. Why was she nervous again? Somehow, she had a bad feeling about this one. It didn't seem to have a return address or company name. It only had Mr. Orzon's name, and nothing else. It was small. Light. Easy for her to carry in one hand. No reason to have a robot carry it, as backup. Isi logged it in with shaking hands. Then, taking a deep breath, she picked it up, and headed for the head office vator. Probably, He would not be in, and she could leave it with the friendly secretary, Isi told herself repeatedly.

The vator ran up, and then over to the main building. Then up again. As before, it stopped two floors below the executive floor. Waiting for permission to go to that floor seemed to take longer, this time. Finally, someone lazily strolled over to her, with a card. Her card seemed to be burning a hole in her pocket. She fished it out, and extended it to the woman, who paid little attention to it.

"Package for the Big Boss, eh?"

"Yes," replied Isi, working hard to appear nonchalant. The woman put both cards into the Executive vator's slot. Other eyes, though, seemed to be boring into her. Why was she going up there? Who was she, anyway? They seemed to ask. Work went on, no matter what the thoughts really were. The vator asked for a thumbprint, once the cards came out. This was the second time that she'd had to go through all of this. It seemed a bit much.

"Next time," the woman said to her, "just your thumbprint will do. They need to know that you are a trusted regular up there, first."

'Unless Mr. Orzon <u>fires</u> me!' Isi said to herself. She hoped that his

suspicions had died down.

Guyan was waiting for her. He knew that this package was coming, as it was from his head agent in The Arrows. Not something for even his secretary to handle. He hoped to find out at last just <u>who</u>, or <u>what</u> The Arrows were looking for, and why that was. Regular mail was safer than the internet. Just an anonymous package. With perhaps Arrows' recruitment stuff, and lots of prayers.

He waited impatiently. Would she still smell of nerves around him? What was she hiding? Being an Arrows' spy? He would check the parcel for tampering, even though there would be no return address. No reason for her to be suspicious of it.

Chapter 9

Isi exited at the top floor. If only Mr. Orzon would <u>not</u> be there! Her heart beat faster. Part of her wanted to see him, though. Just to look at that strong, muscular body and handsome face. That long black hair. She sternly told herself to quit this. He was <u>not</u> for her! He was the head of The ORG. Not someone for a the lowly mailroom clerk that she was now. No matter what she felt about him, he would feel nothing for her, she was sure. Certainly, he wouldn't be out just to receive a parcel.

A robot rolled out to meet her.

"Head office?" she said.

"Follow," it said. Still feeling anxious, Isi cautiously followed it.

Guyan heard and smelled her, as she approached his office. Her fast beating heart, and the combination of anxiety and arousal interested him. Perhaps too much, he told his hardening body. She was his employee. Out of bounds. Clenching his fists, Guyan fiercely reined in his own arousal. His claws starting to come out, causing pain in his palms, at last made him calm a bit. He breathed deeply. Letting his breath out slowly, he got back more control at last.

The secretary's desk was huge. Full of strange 'computery" things that baffled Isi. Why did the office need all of that? Some screens showed views of inner offices, and some showed outside views. All that Isi could see, though, was the tall strong man standing next to the desk. His secretary wasn't there. He was waiting with strangely predatory eyes, set on her rather like a large cat, Isi hysterically thought. Just watching her, silently.

Why did he have to be the only one here? Was he waiting for her, or just for the package? She wondered what was in this package. Why did he seem to still suspect her of something wrong? Isi reminded herself fretfully that she was doing nothing to him, nor to his company. She wasn't sure of exactly what The ORG did, just that she needed to be wary about it, according to her friends at the old, wrecked condo complex.

All that she wanted to do was to escape the Arrows, and be free. To not have to send spirits into the Hell region for silly, small reasons, that the rigid Arrows believed were Evil. She straightened her spine, and stared right back at the intimidating Mr. Orzon. He had no reason to suspect her of trying to hurt him or his company!

Guyan smelled her nerves increase, as she slowly approached him. He almost smiled, though, as he saw her straighten up, and almost glare at him. What was she hiding? Something was making her very nervous. She seemed to be hiding something. Who was she, really? He wished that he could just read her mind. That would be very rude, even if he could actually do that. How else, though, could he find out what she was up to? His frustration increased, until he realized that he might find out a lot from this information package. He wouldn't have to strip her mind bare...which then made him think of striping her body bare. Guyan almost growled at himself. He hoped that the info package would tell him everything about this suspicious, yet strangely sexy woman.

Pretending to not care, he raised his eyebrows at the hesitant Isi. "You have a package there for me?"

Standing as far back as she could, Isi extended the package to Guyan. His lips twitched. He could see how her arm shook a bit, and he almost let her drop it. Their fingers slightly touched, as he finally took the box. Isi's eyes widened, as she felt an "other" sort of presence in him. What could he be? A shapeshifter, like her friends at home? A speaker to spirits, as she was? Hopefully, he couldn't read minds! If only he could be as welcoming as her friends all were! Guyan thumbprinted her tablet, and Isi turned to go. Oddly, she felt reluctant to leave his alarming presence.

"No 'Hello', "Nice day', or "Awful weather?'" she heard him say. She turned a bit.

"H-hello, sir..." she tried to smile, worrying that she just looked crazy, instead.

Guyan frowned. Why had he teased her? Perplexed with himself, he wondered. Certainly, Isi was physically his type, but everything about her screamed that she was hiding something. He narrowed his eyes. Isi gulped. Why did he sound teasing, and then turn out to be angry?

"Hello Isi," came out in a deep, rich voice. It suggested all sorts of things, but not anger. Her black eyes widened, as she bobbled, backing up nervously. Amused, he advanced on her. He looked down at her sleek long hair, now streaked with red and turquoise. Isi stared at her feet, and then up again. She should not act like a shy Arrow girl, she sternly told herself. She looked up into Guyan's eyes. His eyes were a deep black, but seemed to have a gold-green glitter to them. Their eyes locked for endless moments.

Guyan smiled a cat-like smile, then turned and strode away. Isi seemed to see a tail switching a bit, as he walked away. His secretary finally arrived, and smiled somewhat knowingly at both of them. Reddening, Isi gasped, and almost ran from the area.

Once back in his own office, Guyan opened up the package from his agent at the Arrows' headquarters. Maybe at last, the mystery of Isi would be explained. Lately, though, Isi was looking more like any other stylish office worker. He could see Kitzi's touches on her. He grinned about Kitzi—always so sparkly! He wondered what Isi's style really was. The original, rather dowdy clothes, or this new, sexy, colourful, and sometimes subtly sparkly style? He preferred the sexy, but Isi would look good to him dressed in a burlap sack, he knew. He sighed about that truth.

The package contained some Arrow flyers about how great they were as cover, of course. He put the top ones straight into the recycling. Embedded in the middle ones were computer storage tags. He put the first one into his computer.

"Usual silly stuff," he muttered, frustrated. It was about the Arrows' plans to take over the world, forcibly converting everyone to their rigid religion. Taking over governments in North America, to start. It could happen, but was unlikely. They had many convoluted plots to do so, of course. Convoluted, and rather silly. Guyan snorted at some of the plots. He watched the whole thing, though, just in case they had recently come up with any viable plots.

Would the next tag prove that Isi was a spy in his organization? He held his breath, praying to The Creator that it wasn't so. He set the tag into his computer, and watched. This was a personal video, he saw right away.

Hodding Goad, the head of the Arrows, paced around, roaring at someone out of sight. How did Guyan's spy get this video? It was very hard to get, Guyan was sure. He felt very pleased with the spy that he had sent. The man slept around lots, but produced real results. As in this case, probably gotten by sex with someone or other. Guyan grinned at the idea of corrupting an Arrow insider, and watched the grainy video.

"Where is she? I set you to find her, and you haven't even had a hint of where she is???" Goad was obviously consumed with rage about finding this 'she'. "Don't you know," he raged on, "how important she is to our Plan? We have to send those ghosts to Hell! They will warn that stupid Canadian group, otherwise! Will stop our Plan! They all deserve Hell! They weren't Moral in their life choices!" Goad's face was red, and he seemed ready to foam at the mouth. He kept on ranting. About Evil Ghosts, who hadn't followed the strict moral precepts of The Arrows of God. Who had done drugs, were street people, prostitutes, or had just had sex before marrying. Or, had married the 'wrong' sexes. Or felt attracted to the 'wrong' sex.

Guyan felt nauseated by it all. So many of those people had suffered in life, and had turned to alcohol and/or drugs to dull their pain. The Arrows' head felt that they should also suffer in the Afterlife? Would suffer even more in their Afterlives, if The Arrows had their way. Which was why he tried to save those lost souls, whenever he could. It never seemed to be quite enough. Too many still got caught by the Arrows.

It was strange, though, that they were searching for Isi. She was so shy, and not speaking out against them. Never said anything about them at all, in fact. It <u>must</u> be Isi that Goad was ranting about finding. Who else could it be? Why look for her, in particular? They had many trained ghost senders. Why worry about this one quitting their stupid religion? Why was she so important to their plans?

It <u>had</u> to be her, Guyan thought. Isi shows up, with very little background info. No job history, wearing only slightly different clothes than Arrow women wore. And then there were suddenly Arrow 'Recruiters' all over Toronto, and other parts of Canada. And none of them seeming to try very hard to <u>get</u> recruits.

But—why had Isi not told him, Guyan, about her problems? He could hide and protect her better than anyone else. The Arrows had never dared to try to <u>directly</u> confront The ORG. They mainly kept to their enclave in The States, and hardly ever bothered with Canada, even. They seemed quite happy with their power over the U.S.

He would just have to watch Isi even more closely. Try to see just who and what she was. Guyan smiled at the prospect of watching Isi more. That red dress that she had had on today? Whew! A <u>lovely</u> show of legs and curves. He turned to pull up the computer feed from the packages room.

Chapter 10

Hodding Goad paced back and forth angrily. He was ready to <u>kill</u> someone, he felt. How could that silly non-entity <u>Agnes</u> get away from <u>his</u> church? She was their greatest Ghost Speaker, but seemed to have no brains or guts. Just a boring little shy thing, who should have <u>loved</u> the church! Should have been all nuts about it! Why had <u>she</u> wanted to escape? She'd been given <u>everything</u>! Everything!

She'd never had to work at any <u>real</u> job; had had all of her food provided, expensive clothing given to her; and, a big room, all to herself! When all of the other Ghost Speakers had to share their rooms. Ungrateful little <u>tramp</u>! Had she found some Lover to take her in? If she had done that, he would kill her himself, just to send her to <u>Hell</u>, where women who had sex before marriage <u>deserved</u> to <u>be</u>!

His new secretary/assistant watched him calmly. Hodding glared fiercely at him. How could he be so <u>calm</u>? Their world domination plans had been so very disrupted, that Hodding had no idea of how to get back on track! The U.S. government wouldn't trust them if they couldn't even keep one of their top people in hand! Not just quitting— bad enough—but running away and disappearing? Making it look like they had abused her! It would make people suspicious of his church, and worse—suspicious of <u>him</u>!

He turned to his secretary, who sat there saying nothing at all.

"FIND HER!" he ordered.

His secretary bowed his head, still saying nothing. He left to go and work on it. Hodding hoped that he would work on it better than he had been, so far. One secretary had already been fired because of lack of results. This one seemed more eager to please, as well as more gullible. Hodding smirked to himself. Agnes deserved a good beating once she was back here. If she died during it, so much the better, the stupid slut.

Chapter 11

Isi felt nervous. Tonight was the night of Kitzi's big party. She had never been to a mixed party before--had never been to any party, actually. At times, she had had to meet with the other ghost senders for work. They had all been strange and stiff around her. With Hodding Goad watching her every move, and her living separately from them, they were rather afraid to speak to her. Some even seemed to resent her. She was important to the head of their church, and had had her own room.

It hadn't been much of a room. Very small, with one tiny window high up on the wall. It had felt like a prison cell. No place to feel at ease, other than being able to be alone. She had always felt watched there, too.

Whenever she thought about it, Isi felt amazed at herself. She had managed to get out, to get instructions on how to cross the border secretly. To get her tracker out of herself, too. She had even managed to save a bit of money, in cash. No tracking through the banks. How had she done it all? And yet now, she was afraid of a little party, at a real friend's place? Certainly, the unsettling—and sexy—Mr. Orzon would also be there. But somehow, he wasn't nearly as frightening as Hodding Goad had always been. Mr. Orzon might be suspicious of her, but he didn't seem to be about to trap or imprison her in any way.

Isi wondered why her friends here at the "Almosts" complex were so afraid of The ORG, and of Mr. Orzon? Had he actually done anything to them? He seemed to help them, with a food bank close by, that had more than just food. Did they have the wrong information? Was there any way for her to find out?

As she pondered, Isi got ready for the party, with nerves skittering in her. There would be alcoholic drinks, and even marijuana. And also Mr. Orzon, <u>looking</u> at her. <u>Watching</u> her. With his oddly cat-like eyes, and cat-like way of walking. She could do it, though! Isi told herself firmly. No matter <u>who</u> was there, she would have a <u>wonderful</u> time!

The glittery dress chosen by Kitzi for the party certainly helped. It was so sexy on, that Isi almost didn't recognize herself in the mirror. She had put some extra beading on it, in red, to match the streaks in her hair. She felt surprised at how easily she had picked up beading. It felt like she had a memory of watching a grandmotherly person doing it. Just taking it all in. Isi wondered if she had watched her true grandmother beading. She didn't know when she was adopted by the Arrows, or how that had come about. Had her family been <u>that</u> bad? She wished that she had a clear memory of them all.

Completing her outfit were tall, stretchy black boots. They had flashing lights in the high heels. Also Kitzi's choice, of course! Isi grinned at her transformed reflection.

Kaden looked her up and down as she exited her condo. His friendly dog-face smiled, but a bit sadly.

"I wish that I could become totally human again," he said to her. "I could be your date, and see you safely home."

"I wish that you could be my date, too, Kaden! I need a friend there," answered Isi. "Kitzi will be too busy to be with me much, and the <u>boss</u> is going, too! He-he just <u>watches</u> me! Constantly!"

"Now I want to be totally a <u>dog</u>!" Kaden growled. "So that I can bite his...his a-<u>ankles</u>!" Isi grinned at his attempt to not shock her.

"Take care of my little cat-girl. I might end up staying all night, if I can't get a ride home." Isi handed her little black cat over to Kaden. The tiny hand-paws stuck out, to grab onto Kaden's arm. Kaden smiled down at the little fluffed face.

"Of course I'll take good care of Tarene!" he said. "She's so easy to take care of!"

"She climbs a lot!" warned Isi.

Kaden ruffled the black fur. "I just bought her a cat tower. I'll bring it over tonight."

"You <u>spoil</u> her, Kaden!" Kaden just grinned at her. Isi patted her little cat-girl, and turned to go. As she left the safe zone, the gargoyles' eyes gleamed at her, registering her departure. Outside on the street, the Arrow recruiter curled his lip in disgust at her sexy dress, and then turned away from the shocking sight. Isi smiled at his discomfort. At least <u>he</u> wouldn't be watching her suspiciously anymore. She needed to not be seen by any Arrows as one of theirs. Even though wearing something as revealing as this dress was felt very odd, it certainly was worth it.

As she walked, many ghosts streamed around her, touching her coloured front braids and long hair. She ignored them, and hurried along to the subway.

Kitzi's building was fairly tall. About ten stories. The entry lobby had a laser display going among its many plants. Shooting colours rippled around equally colourful guests, all waiting for the elevators. Kitzi welcomed each guest separately, via her entry screen at the building's doors. She was even more colourful and sparkly than usual.

Her apartment said "Kitzi" as well, with abstract art pieces that moved and glittered. She gave Isi a warm hug when she arrived.

"So happy to see you!" exclaimed Kitzi. "The drinks are over there, unless you want to wait for My Robot, 'Bottie', to serve you! Bottie has been very busy tonight!" Isi looked in the direction that Kitzi was motioning to, and saw a 3D band playing old rock'n'roll tunes.

"I was <u>so</u> worried about you, coming from that bad area—and on the TTC, too!" Kitzi continued. "You should have taken a robo-cab. They aren't very expensive! Now, I'll introduce you to a few people!" Kitzi's dress swirled and changed colours as she turned. Isi followed her into the throng. Mr. Orzon was there. She sensed him, somehow. And tried to hide in the crowd. Hiding in the crowd only worked for a short while. Isi sipped at a frothy, fruity drink, and people watched. A bit of a flurry happened, suddenly. Kitzi and a good looking man with long blond hair met each other, and looked starry eyed right away. Jerry beamed at them both from the side.

Isi felt very happy for Kitzi. She had heard all about her strange break up with 'the Poet', in all of its terrible detail. This man looked to be really Kitzi's type. Very stylishly dressed, and just as good looking. They seemed fascinated with each other. Jerry had done well, to introduce them. It was lovely to see a budding romance.

As for Isi, she stayed safely in her corner. Just watching people interact, and flow around her. She had no alcohol in her drink. She might be going home on the subway, and had to stay in control. Getting home safely was a priority. Robo-cabs didn't go into the broken condos area, because of potential tire and suspension damage. She needed to keep her secrets safe, too.

Suddenly, Isi felt eyes staring at her. She looked up, and saw Mr. Orzon across the room, with an unfathomable look on his face. He began to walk towards her, through the crowded party. Isi gulped. There were no places to hide. The bathroom was too far from her corner. Of course, what could he do to her <u>here</u>? He had never done a thing to her at work, when it was just herself and him in his office. He was even getting friendlier towards her, and less suspicious. Why was she so nervous and tense?

Guyan stood looking down at Isi's bowed head, as she nervously sipped at her drink. She had a sexy, sparkly dress on that showed her thighs at its sides. It all turned his brain to mush, while another part of him went too hard. He glared, feeling angry at himself for lack of control, and Isi flinched. Immediately, he felt remorse. It wasn't her fault. Others had less clothing on, after all. What <u>was</u> it about <u>her</u>, in particular? He wanted to touch her. To comfort her fears—of himself!--and stroke her shining black hair. Tonight, a lit up strip of red shone in her braids. It matched the red beading around the dress collar. Guyan tried hard to not look lower than her collar.

Finally, Isi got the courage to look up at him. What was he angry about? She had been invited to Kitzi's party, too! He had been right there, when both of them were invited! And Kitzi knew <u>her</u> a lot better than she knew Mr. Orzon. She and Kitzi had become good friends, even.

Forgetting that he was her boss, Isi glared back at Guyan.

Guyan's lips twitched suddenly. It was like having a small kitten hissing and trying to scratch at him. He couldn't help but to let his eyes rove over her with real appreciation. Isi blushed, and again looked down. She felt so <u>exposed</u> in this dress! Finally, his eyes left her, as he looked at the commotion over Kitzi and the blond man. Both of them were staring at each other with stunned and awestruck expressions.

Jerry was there, speaking to them both, but they were too involved with each other to notice him. Jerry grinned, giving up. Isi looked up, as the room went a bit quiet. She saw that somehow, a glow was radiating from both of them. Her eyes widened.

"Love at first sight," she murmured. She had always wondered if such a thing truly existed, and here was proof! Obvious to everyone. To her, even more obvious. She could plainly see the glows emanating from each one of them, and seeming to touch and merge together.

Guyan smelled pheromones hot and heavy in the air. He looked down again at Isi. Who was actually looking happy, instead of nervous for a change. Suddenly, he wanted her. All of her. His teeth elongated in his mouth, and he pulled them back before they could be seen. What she had murmured sank in suddenly.

"Do you believe in love at first sight? That," he stated, waving his arm at the glowing couple, "<u>That</u> could be <u>lust</u> at first sight!"

"I believe <u>now</u> in love at first sight," Isi finally said.

"What about it convinced you?" Guyan looked down at her, puzzled. Isi shut her lips firmly, not wanting to say what she had *seen*. "<u>Well</u>?" he demanded.

"They don't just have looks of lust!" she finally answered. "Look at their <u>expressions</u>!"

Guyan sensed that she had seen more than just expressions, but wondered if he should just drop the subject. He needed to talk about <u>something</u>, though, since he had come over to her. Couldn't just stand there, feeling and looking stupid. Somehow, it was very hard to leave her side. He began to talk of the party, and Kitzi's robot. Love seemed to be a good topic to avoid, when it came to her. Isi answered easily, and they had a real conversation for the first time. Guyan was careful to not ask about her past, so that she'd not fearfully clam up on him. Instead, he told her a few funny stories about himself, and actually got some smiles, and even a small chuckle from her. In return, Isi told him about her mischievous climbing kitten—<u>without</u> the hand-paws detail. He certainly felt relieved that she liked cats.

Time passed quickly, as they spoke of beliefs and other things. She was not a prejudiced sort of person, and accepted all religions. She knew nothing of her Indigenous family, or their beliefs, it seemed. Guyan felt sad for her, having missed so much of her culture and heritage. Who had brought her up? Isi wouldn't say. That was also sad, he thought. That she had no happy family to mention.

The party was starting to wind down, Isi noticed when she looked around. She had been so absorbed in the conversation with Mr. Orzon, that the time had flown by. She could see Kitzi's cute little robot collecting glasses and plates. Kitzi and her new love sat and stared deeply into each others' eyes.

After breaking off the fascinating conversation with Mr. Orzon, (he had told her to call him Guyan, but that felt a bit odd), Isi went up to Kitzi.

"I'm leaving now, Kitzi. Thanks so much for inviting me to your wonderful party!" Isi smiled at Kitzi, as she looked up with vague, dreamy eyes.

"Oh! Do you have a ride home, or should I call you a robo-cab?" asked Kitzi.

The robo-cabs wouldn't go to Isi's area, because of the broken up roads. The subway actually went closer to her home.

"I'm fine, Kitzi. I have a ride," Isi lied. She blushed, hoping that Kitzi couldn't tell that she was lying.

"Oh! That's great! And, I forgot—this is Apollo, Isi!" Isi smiled at the man, who actually suited his grandiose name. He smiled happily back, with as dreamy an expression as Kitzi had had. Kitzi stood up, and hugged Isi. "Have a safe trip home! I'll see you Monday!" Isi smiled and nodded at the glowing couple, and then left.

Once outside, she began to walk. Now, where was that subway entrance again? It was hard to remember in the dark. She suddenly shivered, but told herself that it was a safe neighbourhood. What could she be worried about? Nobody was following her! She looked behind her anyway, and a large dark person loomed.

"eek!" she squeaked, and then the large and scary person turned slowly into Guyan.

"What are you doing?" he growled. "Where is your robo-cab?"

"I-I w-was looking for the subway," Isi stammered her reply. "I—it's a long trip, and I can't really...aff--"

"I'll drive you home, then," Guyan interrupted.

"Oh no, you shouldn't! I can't impose..." but Guyan firmly took her arm in his large hand, guiding her.

"Just drive me to the closest subway station, please," Isi nervously managed to say. "It's, ah, kind of hard to get to by car..." She stumbled off the subject, as Guyan brought her to a luxurious aero-car. "Oh." Her eyes widened.

"No problem for <u>this</u> car!" Guyan smugly said to her. He suddenly felt suspicious of her again. Was she trying to hide that she had a place with The Arrows? He looked down at her nervous face, wondering. He still wasn't sure of what she was hiding. He believed that she had escaped The Arrows, but did he just <u>want</u> to believe that, or was it the truth? He would definitely follow her, once she was out of his car. See where she <u>really</u> went.

For most of the way, they flew just above the regular roads. The easy conversation of the party wasn't there anymore. Isi again felt nervous, and she saw Guyan glancing suspiciously at her once again. The tangled mess of the old condos came up, and Guyan prepared to turn from them, but Isi pointed to their centre.

Guyan's eyebrows rose up, but then he frowned with confusion. No Arrow office could be there. No Arrows would be brave enough to actually <u>live</u> among the odd people who lived here. Saying nothing, he flew until he saw a small area that seemed to be mostly free of debris.

"I can get out here," Isi said to him. "It's safe from here."

Guyan could see eyes looking at them, some glowing in the dark, as they heard the sound of his rotors.

"I will see you <u>safely</u> to your door!" he snapped, feeling worried.

He looked sternly at Isi.

"No!" Isi blurted out, alarmed. He narrowed his black eyes at her, and Isi thought that she saw a flash of gold glinting in them.

"I mean--i-it's OK,....sir..." she stammered out.

The eyes surrounding them came closer.

Chapter 8

His expensive car did not belong in their territory. Guyan smelled
shapeshifters and drugs in the air. Isi, though, opened her door, and she
—What???--<u>WAVED</u>??? Guyan opened his door, starting to come out,
but low growls stopped him. Too many for him to fight alone. Isi said
nothing as she left him there. She confidently strode though the pack of
eyes, to a very dark doorway. At the doorway, eerie red lights seemed
to scan her. Strange to have real security in <u>this</u> area, thought Guyan.

Isi acted as though it was all very normal, and even boring. She
turned around, and waved at him, then just disappeared into the depths
of the dark and forbidding doorway.

Well, she certainly seemed to live <u>here</u>. Guyan felt like telling her
off. Why live in such a bad area? Didn't he pay her enough to afford a
<u>real</u> apartment? He grumbled to himself as his aero car lifted off, and
left the shattered area. If only he had the right to say such things to her!
They had gotten along so well at the party, but then he let his suspicions
get in the way of them becoming truly friendly. He should <u>not</u> have
such strong feelings for an employee of his! It was so <u>stupid</u> of him!
Guyan turned on his auto-pilot, and ordered his car home, so that he
could rant to himself even more.

Isi was telling herself the same sorts of things. How could she be <u>so</u>
attracted to her <u>boss</u>? Sure, he was very handsome and intelligent, and
he seemed to be kind, as well. She had never heard any of his
employees complain about him. He seemed to be liked by all. In fact,

she had even noticed a few women looking jealously at her, whenever she had to speak to him. She wasn't the only one to have developed a crush on him, yet she still felt rather silly to have done so.

She still didn't know why her friends here at home had warned her about him and The ORG. She would ask Kaden –tomorrow. Tonight, she felt too confused and tired. Tired from the late night, and confused by Guyan's worry about her safety.

*   *   *

Hodding paced, agitatedly. If Agnes wasn't found <u>soon</u>, his whole church could be in jeopardy. She was his <u>best</u> ghost-speaker! And so many souls were building up, destined for Hell! His other ghost-speakers couldn't seem to nudge <u>any</u> of them over. He just knew that Agnes could do that. She practically saw the ghosts as solid people, after all!

Yet, she had never even <u>tried</u> to send any of those Evil Prostitutes and Addicts to Hell! He had just been lecturing her on her Duty to do so, and then she up and disappeared. If Agnes wasn't found soon, more of those Evil ones would be saved, and sent to <u>Heaven</u>, instead! The more powerful Ghost speakers at The ORG would do that. They had no concept of True Right and Wrong.

Hodding ground his teeth.

Also, if anyone ever found out that Agnes had been kidnapped from a Native family, his church would go up in flames. If those now influential Indian tribes found out that she had been scooped from Canada's Indigenous peoples, because of her ability to see ghosts at a very young age, governments would be all over them! Prying into their finances, and <u>all</u>! Hodding wished for the old days, when Indians got ignored, and left to disappear., along with their awful religions. All of the big churches had apologized like crazy, instead. Hodding ground his teeth again.

She <u>had</u> to be found, and brought back! Even if they had to chain her to her bed. Her being free, and possibly remembering, and talking, could not be risked. The media would be all over it! People would leave his church in <u>droves</u>, and <u>he</u> might even be <u>jailed</u>! He; the most <u>Righteous</u> man in the <u>world</u>! Jailed! <u>He</u> was a <u>Godly</u> man! He should be <u>praised</u>, for having taken Agnes away from her Heathen family! He had saved her soul! Had taught her the True Word of God. How could those Unbelievers be allowed to put <u>him</u> on trial!

<u>God</u> would not allow it!!

While raging inside, Hodding ordered his secretary to send off angry emails to all of his searchers. His secretary watched him silently, as he typed. A buzzer went off. It was the sound of one of his few outlying recruiters.

"Yes! Report!" Hodding ordered.

"Master!" an excited voice answered.

"Report!" Hodding again ordered.

"A girl with long black hair was seen in The Condo District last night."

"What is the Condo District?" he asked, pulling up his map of Toronto.

"Waterfront. Old, broken down condo towers."

"Ah, I see. Who is posted there?"

"Only one or two youngsters. It's not a good recruiting area. Rough. A good place for her to hide in. Nobody asks questions there, I hear."

"I will go, then."

"It's supposed to be dangerous--" the voice said, with some hesitation.

"Then you, and some picked members will go with me! We will extract her from this Evil Place," Hodding proclaimed confidently. "Such <u>low</u> people won't be able to stop <u>us</u>!"

The outlier agreed.

And the secretary typed on, saying nothing.

Chapter 12

Isi was busy punching in mail and packages, when the board lit up with a face to face call. Tentatively, she answered. Guyan's face seethed out at her.

"Report to my office!" he snapped, and the connection cut off.

"What will I do?" she asked the walls.

"Work?" a voice answered her. She jumped a bit, then realized that of course it was one of the resident ghosts. She frowned in its direction, but said nothing. Guyan might see her apparently talking to herself. And she must already be in some sort of trouble. What had she done?, Isi wondered.

It seemed to be something very serious, and Isi wracked her brain. She hadn't had much time to do anything this week. The day had just started, and Guyan had been so friendly at the party only two days ago. Perhaps he had heard something bad about her? From one of those jealous girls? Would she lose her job over something untrue? How could she prove that it wasn't true, whatever it was? She began to add up her saved money in her head, as she prepared to go to head office.

At least, by living in the ruined condos, she had no rent expenses. As well, she grew a lot of her own food. The only expensive things were her new clothes. They had taken a chunk out of her salary and savings. She could live for a few months on what was left, still. She would eventually want a new job, to get a nicer place. Today, she might be looking for a new job.

Too soon, the head offices were ahead of her. Why did the vators go so fast? Nervously, she approached the empty secretary's desk.

Guyan's office door was closed. She heard the voice of the secretary inside. Should she wait? Or knock? Isi shuffled her feet nervously, and waited. The voices continued on.

After several minutes, Isi gave up, and went to the door. Hesitantly, she knocked. At least this way, she'd not have to be alone with the strangely angry Guyan. The door opened.

Guyan was standing behind his desk. His secretary stood in front, with some papers. Guyan seemed to resemble a cat more than ever. His eyes seemed to shine golden. Isi could swear that she saw a shadowy tail swishing angrily back and forth behind him. They stared at each other for moments, as his secretary shuffled papers.

"Sir, is there a problem with my work?..." Isi trailed off, as Guyan still said nothing. He just stared at her with narrowed eyes for several minutes.

Isi began to tremble a bit, as Guyan strode over to her, and loomed. What could be that bad? She tried to feel angry at him, but it just fizzled out.

"Why—WHY do you live in a SLUM!" Guyan hissed the words out.

Isi wished that he hadn't loomed at her, but she slowly began to feel angry at him at last. It was none of his business!

"Don't I pay you enough? Are you just hoarding money? Are you giving money to some stupid religious cult? What are you doing there?" Guyan's intense eyes bored into Isi.

"I—I--I--" Isi stuttered to a stop, gulping. But suddenly, words seemed to burst out of her. "I don't know what business it is of yours, where I choose to live! Or, what I choose to do with MY MONEY!" she almost yelled. Where did those words come from? she wondered.

"Who are you giving it to?" demanded Guyan.

"NOBODY!"

Guyan's eyes narrowed into cat slits, a hysterical part of Isi said to her. "Then you hoard it?" he said sarcastically.

"No! I—sometimes I give it to people around there. People who need help."

"Those <u>Arrow</u> recruiters?" Guyan hissed.

"God, no! <u>Not</u> to <u>them</u>!" Isi exclaimed. "Never to <u>them</u>," she said under her breath. Guyan heard her muttered afterthought, and knew that she spoke the truth. Some of his rage abated. At least she also did not like the Arrows. More and more, he was seeing that she must be the one that they were frantically searching for. He looked at Isi with frustration.

"Why are you living there?" It's certainly not safe!"

"It <u>is</u> safe!" argued Isi. "For me, it is <u>very</u> safe!" She could hardly believe that she was actually arguing with her boss! Why was she doing this? She was yelling at the head of the company! Her-a mailroom clerk! And telling him things that he probably should not be told. Where was her head at? Frantically, she looked around, wondering if she would see something possessing her. All that she could see was the secretary outside, working at something, while pretending to not see or hear a thing.

And, of course, she saw Guyan in front of her. He was now looking at her in a bemused sort of way, with an oddly soft look in his usually feral and fierce eyes.

He gently said, "I'm sorry. It really <u>isn't</u> my business at all. I was just worried about you. Go back to work." He turned, with his long braid swinging, and went back to his desk.

Isi stood there, stunned at the sudden apology, and his softness towards her, then finally turned to leave.

Chapter 13

Guyan resolved to keep a better eye on Isi, even though he was less worried about her living arrangement. She trusted her neighbourhood, even though he couldn't see why that was. He worried about the Arrows finding her, even in that unlikely spot. Who could protect her there?

He asked Jerry to watch out for her, as his large wolf self. Jerry reported that Isi seemed to be well liked in the rough area; that she was well protected there. Any men trying to accost her seemed to be frightened off by strange things happening to them. Bricks would fly around, sometimes hitting the men bothering Isi.

Jerry was worried about the single Arrow recruiter in the area, though. That man seemed to be watching her closely, which was unusual for just a recruiter.

Guyan decided to check things out for himself. He slipped around buildings, unseen, trying to listen to any words in the air. Then heard the Arrow recruiter speaking to a higher up—and obviously about Isi. Seemed that she had started out in the area wearing long, loose clothing, but had changed her style more and more, into sexy and short. It seemed suspicious to the recruiter, and confirmed Guyan's guess that she was trying to escape the Arrows. But why were they so after her? Why was Isi so important to them?

Later, sitting on top of a wall, he again heard the recruiter softly speaking into his hidden mic. Guyan carefully padded forward, and looked at the recruiter.

"She's going into her building now. It is 5:28 p.m." the recruiter softly breathed into his mic. Guyan took note, as with everything to do with Isi.

Wanting to protect her, Guyan kept up his patrols. He walked along tops of crumbling high walls, unseen and unheard, he believed. He now always followed Isi home, to be sure that she was safely back in her gargoyle protected condo building.

Guyan began to try harder to gain Isi's trust. He spent several days, just talking with her. She was still not telling him of her past, or what she was doing in Toronto. But, he could see her relaxing more and more around him. They had great discussions about everything in life. For some reason, she never would speak of her beliefs about death and the afterlife. Guyan was patient, and only spoke softly to her. He dreamed of one day actually going somewhere with her. Of them being just themselves, not boss and employee. Until then, he would continue to protect her, at least. He would find out why the Arrows were looking so hard for her.

Chapter 11

Isi could sense someone following her. She felt that it was Guyan, and wondered why. Was he still suspicious of her, even though lately they had been getting along very well? They often just talked, when she had to go to his office. He even at times came to the mail room, and just wanted to be around her, it seemed. They talked about everything, it seemed. From politics to the environment, to Indigenous issues and events. She looked forward to one day going to a powwow. Guyan had said that he danced, and she would love to see that, she thought. Was he still not trusting her? She was still afraid to let him know of her past with the Arrows, and her escape from them. More and more, though, she wondered about her neighbours' fear of Guyan and The ORG.

Could they all be wrong? Why were they all so afraid of The ORG? It could be because they were shifters who were stuck between forms, Isi thought. Many would not approve of how they got to be that way, but Guyan seemed to be quite open-minded about most things. He never seemed to blame people for drug habits, so why blame shifters who were stuck only because of their former drug habits? Guyan was a proud Indigenous man, and certainly knew the history of many Indigenous people getting addicted to drink and drugs because of pain in their souls. Even though these shifters were mostly white, Isi felt certain that Guyan would be compassionate about anyone's pain leading them into addictions.

As she made her way home, she pondered these things, and wondered if she should get Guyan and her friends to meet. But, she also wondered why Guyan kept on following her home. It was irritating! She had come all of the way here, by hopping a freight train, and he thought that she couldn't take care of herself? Or, he was just still very suspicious of her? Isi felt angry, when she thought of it all. Maybe tomorrow, she would shake him off. Get off at another stop, and prove to him, and to herself, that she could take care of herself very well. She decided to wear lower heeled shoes tomorrow. One never knew. She still needed to be careful. She would prove to Guyan that she could take care of herself!

The next day, again, she had a wonderful talk with Guyan. It made her wonder about her suspicions of his motives. He was so at ease with her, now. Was he the one following her at all? He seemed to have no inclination to follow her around. He seemed to just be friendly and interested in what she had to say. What if it was actually an Arrow person following her? Isi thought hard all day about what to do. Should she trust Guyan, and let him protect her, thinking that it was him? Or should she try to escape her mysterious follower?

She wrote the pros and cons, and got nowhere. She went through the rest of her day in a daze of confusion, but somehow made no mistakes. No one said that any parcels had gotten to the wrong places, at least. Shaking her head at her confusion, she said a hopefully cheery goodbye to Kitzi, and logged off for the day. She got into her new fall coat, and the low boots that she had brought, and headed out, still unsure of what stop she would get off at.

While reading her escapist book on the subway train, Isi became aware that it had stopped longer than usual at one stop before hers. It made up her mind. She would get off here. It was meant to be. Almost reluctantly, she gathered up her purse and reader, and exited the train.

This was a more dangerous area, but perhaps it would have been even more dangerous to let whoever it was to follow her again. If it was Guyan, after all, he might find out too much about her, Isi reflected. Her mind was so confused about him! He seemed nice and safe, and some of her friends at home now thought that Guyan might be the only person who could truly help her to live normally, and not in hiding anymore. Others, though, still warned her of him, and of The ORG. Isi felt so safe with him. Too safe, perhaps. Was it only because of her attraction to him, though? She needed this time to be just alone, to think. To not be wondering if someone was following her, and to not have to hear conflicting advice about him. Isi relaxed, as she ambled her way through broken streets and buildings. She smiled to see the green poking through, as nature took over this part of the city. She left her confused thoughts and longings about the head of the company behind, for a short while.

Then, she began to wonder again. Did he truly look at her like he felt some attraction, too? Was she just seeing what she wished to see? She was just a lowly file and mail clerk, after all. How could the head of the company see her in that way? All of her confusion made her nervous and often unable to think coherently, when around him. She found herself wishing that he was not her boss, and had nothing to do with The ORG. Then, she could be at ease with him, and be more able to enjoy their good conversations whenever they happened to meet each other.

Isi shook her head, trying to shake away the thoughts of her too handsome boss. She had to be alert here. This condo area was much more broken down and dreary than her own area. Shadowy figures seemed to lurk in doorways and dark alleys. Dirt swirled around everyone. She quickened her steps, now aware of hostile feelings directed her way. She was dressed too well for this tattered and sad area. A tattered figure, with a long dirty beard loomed out of one of the dark alleys, and pointed at her accusingly.

"REPENT!" he yelled. "The Arrows of God command you whores to REPENT!" spittle foamed out of his mouth, as his yellowed old eyes gleamed with fanaticism.

Isi carefully walked around him, trying hard to not breathe in his terrible smell. She also avoided looking at him, hoping that he would then leave her be. So, did not see the sudden gleaming of actual intelligence in his fanatical eyes.

She was out of sight and hearing when he muttered into his filthy

collar.

"Looks like her. Condo district, area one. Heading east."

Chapter 14

Finally, Isi had begun to to get close to her own area. There was one last tunnel to traverse. She hurried through it, into the labyrinth of the adjacent area. She felt eyes staring at her, but dismissed them as just curious about her. She had gotten through the worst condo areas safely. She could start to relax now.

As she hurried past the alleys, she never noticed the dark figures gathering in them. Waiting for her to pass, they then began to stealthily follow her into the depths. She felt an itching sense of something, but saw nothing unusual. Could she just be nervous because she was closer to home, and couldn't quite believe her luck at being safe?

Suddenly, a spirit jumped in front of her.

"Aaaa!" Isi gasped, as her heart also jumped. She had not even been thinking of spirits, let alone trying to contact any! She felt slightly annoyed. She had no time now to help any spirits to cross over. This area was too unknown, and could be dangerous. She just wanted to see her friendly gargoyles, and be safely at home with her little cat-girl. She still stopped, though, and began to meditate, so as to open a door to the Beyond.

"NO!!" the rather raggedy looking spirit yelled at her. Isi jumped a bit, surprised. She opened her eyes, and stared at the spirit, surprised at his outburst. "Others! Arrows! They're after you! RUN!" the spirit beckoned to her, and then went into a dark passageway. Hesitantly, Isi followed. Wasn't this even worse? She wondered.

Again, the spirit motioned to her. "Faster! You need to RUN!" Then, she heard the sounds of many boots, heading in her direction. She ran into a dark maze of fallen rubble, consisting of bricks, broken concrete, and glass. She had to work hard to not trip. Her boot heels were not as easy to run in as she'd thought. Low heels, but not low enough.

"This way!" a rough voice yelled behind her. Too close! Gasping, Isi kept on running, following the spirit. Putting her head down, she sped up as much as she could.

Guyan was worried and upset. Where was Isi? She had not come out of her regular subway stop, and he hadn't seen her anywhere along her usual route home. He paced back and forth, growling to himself. Should he leave here, while she might get into trouble? Or should he go to see if she had somehow slipped by him, to get home early? He decided to to go to her home, just to check if she was already there, and safe. He contacted Jerry to cover for him, and impatiently waited for him to arrive. As soon as Jerry arrived, he shot out of his concealing building, and ran in cat form to Isi's condo building.

At the condo, the eyes of the two gargoyles were spinning around, while shooting out strange rays. Guyan stood well back, wondering what was going on. He changed back to human, and quickly put on some jeans. How could he get into her building, to ask anyone? Was it a wasted trip? He fumed and paced.

Then, two strange shape shifters came rushing out. They were not totally turned! How had that happened? He approached them.

"What is going on? Why haven't you two completed your shifts?" he demanded. They both jumped, and huddled together, obviously afraid of him. Guyan just looked at them, not moving again. Finally, the dog-headed one tentatively told him that they were stuck in those forms. Not extremely surprised, because that did happen at times— either from trauma or an addiction, or both—Guyan said nothing. He just nodded with sympathy, and quietly asked if Isi had returned home yet.

"No," the dog-headed one replied. "And both of us seem to be almost seeing a ghost, trying to tell us something about her! We *feel* that it has to do with Isi, anyway!"

"Where is this spirit?" asked Guyan, and suddenly, the gargoyles' fulminating eyes seemed to catch a wavering 3-D image of a tattered old beggar.

Closing his eyes, Guyan concentrated on the spirit, and heard him say, "She's in trouble! The Arrows are closing in on her!"

"WHERE?" Guyan yelled frantically, echoed by both of the others.

"Follow me!" and the 3-D image went transparent, but could still be seen by Guyan as a shimmer in the air. Swiftly, Guyan removed his jeans, leaving just a black stretch outfit on, and he changed into a large mountain lion. Motioning to the two stuck in phase shifters, he ran after the shimmering spirit. Somehow, both men dropped to all fours, and a hound and a raccoon emerged totally. The hound howled and the raccoon growled and screeched. They followed behind the big cat, along with a murky cloud of other spirits. All of them determined to help Isi.

In a dark alley, they finally saw her, running frantically, tripping and sliding along. Yet somehow, Isi was able to keep ahead and out of sight of a large group of men charging in heavy boots behind her. The men were followed by a panting older man, who looked angry. Guyan leapt to the top of a roof, to keep Isi in sight, then changed back to human. All of this shifting back and forth was making him slightly dizzy, but he knew that he could not take on all of those men alone. Panting, he contacted his squad for support, and then the police, to wait to see if any arrests would be needed. He hoped that there would be <u>many</u> arrests!

Isi kept on running, hoping to outpace the massed Arrow men. She was amazed that she had done so, so far. Maybe she could outrun them all of the way home? But, what then? They would know where she lived! Would she ever be free, and able to go out ever again? Her breath sobbed in and out, and things blurred from tears. She kept on running, head down to see what she could on the ground.

Up on a roof, and behind the massed men of the Arrows, Guyan's eyes gleamed. Once his squad arrived, he joined in the chase; motioning with its head and chirping to a group of other large cats. Several wolves stayed back within the ruins, so as to not be seen or heard. The cats jumped from beam to beam, and from crumbling rooftops to broken walls, following Isi and the running men.

Isi had to stop. She could not see the spirit any longer. Somehow, he had gotten too far ahead of her. She looked around her, as she tried to catch her breath. Which way was best? She saw a larger opening on the right. That might lead to a street, and easier going. Was it wise to go to a street, though? Or should she keep to the hidden ways, still? She couldn't hesitate for long. She could still hear feet running behind her, even though she seemed to have lost them for a bit.

She took another long breath, and then turned and ran right. Her feet could not take the broken up concrete any longer. Her soft leather boots were getting shredded, and she thought that she could see traces of blood on the sides. She felt blisters coming up, as well.

The leading man of the Arrows got a glimpse of black hair blowing back, and he pointed.

"RIGHT!" he yelled.

They were getting closer! Isi tried to run faster, tripping often in her heels. <u>Why</u> did she buy such <u>silly</u> boots? Just because they were <u>sexy</u>? To impress <u>who</u>? Guyan, of course! Did he notice them? Probably not! She somehow managed to get a bit farther ahead, and saw a small alley opening up. She charged into it.

Into—a dead end cul-de-sac, full of rusted cast iron benches, and a few scraggly trees. Desperately, she ran around the small area, looking for a passage out. There <u>HAD</u> to be one!

"<u>There</u> you are!" the smarmy voice belonged to the leading Arrow. <u>Too</u> many Arrows swarmed in behind him, overpowering the small space with their bulk and weapons. Isi backed up against a wall. Would they shoot her?

A man with a dark, angry face set in stone, followed the armed Arrow thugs. He began to circle around the space, moving in on Isi. He glared at her.

"Agnes. It is time for you to come home."

"NO!" Isi yelled. "It's not my home! It never has been! You stole me from my real family!"

"It is your only home, Agnes! Who else would want a freak like you, but us? Talking to ghosts? Evil ones, even? You had to be taught to send them where they belonged! In Hell! We could NOT let your pagan family keep such a talent!" Hodding Goad was shouting by the end of his tirade. Isi could see bits of foam coming out of his raging mouth. She held herself straight, refusing to shake with fear.

She held up her head proudly, looking him in the eyes.

"My name is not Agnes," she calmly stated. "It is Aiyana. The name that my real family gave to me!"

"Idolators! Pagans! Savages!" Hodding spat out.

Unnoticed by both antagonists, on the rooftop Guyan changed from his cougar form, back to human. He was covered in a black, stretchy, and breathable one piece, with a hole for his tail in the back. A stretch harness was clipped to his back, containing regular clothes. A small mic picked up his softly spoken words, sending them to the surrounding wolves and the other cats. A Toronto police team waited for more word to move in, as the shape shifters swiftly closed in on the little parkette.

Hard-eyed, Hodding advanced on Isi. "I am the head of The Arrows of God, and I say that you belong to us! You will submit, as a proper woman should!"

"NO!" Isi cried out, but he grabbed her arm painfully. She struggled to escape, but another very large man came up behind her, and grabbed her by the waist, and over her other arm, as she poised to scratch at Hodding. Isi screamed loudly. Perhaps someone around here would come to help her? A large hand came around her mouth. She bit down on it, but seemingly not hard enough. The hand stayed. She bit again, and he swore, taking it away for an instant. Isi screamed again.

"Get the rope!" Hodding called out. "And a gag!"

Another one of his followers came up, holding a rough, thick rope, and a dirty piece of cloth.

That was enough for Guyan. He quickly changed back to his mountain lion form, and dropped down--right on top of Hodding Goad. Hodding screamed as he was knocked over. He stared, terrified, into the eyes of the big cat. Suddenly, there was a bright light, and Guyan's human form materialized, still holding down Hodding by his shoulders.

The man holding Isi let his hands go limp, and Isi pulled away from him, as he stared, horrified, at Guyan. Other large cats had landed next to the other Arrow thugs, and had also turned into men. The thugs shook, and stood silently, watching Guyan and Hodding.

"Assault! Assault!" Hodding yelled out. "You will go to jail for this, you Evil Creature!"

"No," Guyan replied shortly. "You will go, Asshole. It's all on tape. Attempted abduction of a very unwilling person."

"She is one of us! She has to come home!"

"She is an adult, and can decide on her own. Nobody can force her!"

Isi then heard what she had only vaguely noticed before. Howling. Close by. Suddenly, the small parkette was full of massive wolves. Many of them were wearing police vests. Also, some of the cougars wore police vests. Police also jumped out of the buildings and the alley, and ran with the wolves, circling around everyone. They removed handcuffs from backpacks, and cuffed all of the men held down by wolves and cougars.

Behind them, Isi heard baying and growling. She looked, and saw a large hound and raccoon run into the parkette. Somehow, they seemed familiar...

Then, a police flyer landed; the trussed up Arrows were bundled into it. Guyan turned to her, as Hodding Goad, the head of The Arrows of God—the man that she had feared for so very long—was also loaded up into the large police flyer. Wide-eyed, she took in his muscular physique, in his skin-tight outfit. Even in shock, her body responded to his.

Guyan smirked for a few seconds, but then his face turned stern. "I think that you can now begin to explain yourself, Isi—beginning with your real name," he quietly said, arms folded.

"I---I---I--..."Isi shook with reaction. She could not believe that it was all over, and had happened so fast, as well.

Guyan's eyes suddenly softened. He took in her messy hair, her scuffed clothes, and her bleeding feet; barely protected by her soft leather boots, with their heels falling off. Walking over to her, he put his arms around her carefully.

"Don't you ever scare me like that again, my love," he gently said.

"L—lo--"

Guyan held her gently for a few moments, then he picked up the bedraggled Isi/Aiyana/Agnes?, and he strode away with her through the broken glass, metal, and concrete. Somehow, he had acquired boots, when Isi was distracted by the hound and raccoon pair. Before they left, she looked at them again. Could they be Kaden and Rob? Actually fully *changed*? She began to smile, and Guyan smiled back at her. She looked up at his wonderful, strong, and handsome face and long black hair. Tentatively, she touched his face, and then buried her face in his shoulder, embarrassed. She did feel safe, at last.

Guyan kissed her nose, smiling at her.

"It's all over now," he said. "Yes, I do love you. Only, I don't see why! You are such a pain! Whatever your name really is!"

"Aiyana!" Aiyana—no longer Isi, and certainly not Agnes!—firmly told him.

"Your true last name is what, then?" Guyan asked softly.

"I—I really don't remember. I was so young, when taken by the Arrows," she looked down, ashamed. Could her parents have given her up?

"We will find your true family!" Guyan vowed. No one should be brought up by the Arrows, let alone a sensitive spirit walker like Aiyana was.

"Wh-what if they gave me up?" Aiyana stammered out.

"Didn't you hear that idiot say that the Arrows couldn't let someone like you, with your talent, stay with your family?" Guyan reminded her, gently. "What exactly is your talent?"

Eyes wide, Aiyana looked up at Guyan's handsome, caring face, and answered him. "I can clearly see and speak to spirits, and send them on."

"A true Spirit Walker," Guyan breathed. "You could always do this?"

"Yes, since I was a small child. Does it matter to you?" Aiyana asked worriedly.

"It is wonderful!" he grinned. "The ORG needs someone like you!"

"What do you need me for? I won't be sending undeserving spirits to Hell!" Aiyana glared. Guyan grinned, and squeezed her.

"We try to get the troubled spirits before The Arrows do, to send them to good places. I can do it, and so can many in our squad, but it is draining, and hard for us to contact the spirits, let alone send them on. It is the main reason for The ORG. We aren't just for doing data for other companies!" he answered her.

Aiyana's face glowed with joy, and Guyan caught his breath at her beauty. She touched his face with wonder.

"I ended up in the right place!"

"You certainly did!" he answered, "And now you are promoted to the squad, but still will do your other duties, as all of us do ours. You are one of us, now, Aiyana!" Guyan kissed her soft lips.

EPILOGUE

Chanting and the drum filled the air. Aiyana and Guyan stood holding hands, as The Grand Entry went by them. Her feet wanted to dance to the rhythm of the Earth. Dancers and elders were announced loudly.

"Do you ever dance?" she quietly asked Guyan.

"Often. I love to dance," answered Guyan. "To celebrate my culture. Today, though, I am with you. My mother and sisters will teach you to dance, as well. Very soon. Then we'll teach our children."

Aiyana looked down, blushing at the thought of their children. She could then see the little now almost human face of Tarene, her little cat-baby. A good future. Guyan tilted her head up, and smiled deeply into her eyes. He could hardly believe his good luck, in finding and getting such a prize woman. Lovely, loving, caring, and so strong. Not bitter from her ordeal of a life with the Arrows. He was angered even more at Hodding Goad, having heard of how Aiyana had lived with them. It certainly was not the family atmosphere that they bragged about to the public. Not for Aiyana.

It was now established that Aiyana had been stolen from her family. The trial of Hodding Goad was ongoing. He was charged by both the Canadian and American governments, for stealing her as a very young child, and then again trying to kidnap her as an adult.

"I hope that my own family can be found," Aiyana said quietly.

"We will find them! They have probably been looking for you for a long time!" Guyan firmly told her. She smiled at him with gratitude and happiness.

Suddenly, she grinned at something beyond Guyan.

"What?!" he asked.

"Look!" She nodded her head in that direction, and he turned around, to see Jerry and Kaden also watching the Grand Entry. They also were holding hands.

After their sudden shifts to hound and raccoon, Guyan had taken both Kaden and Rob in hand, and had taught them how to shift properly again. Their fears of being scorned by other shifters were baseless, as Aiyana had thought. Somehow, though, Kaden still seemed to have a face like a hound. Jerry obviously didn't mind. She was happy to see her friends now attached. Well, except for Rob. He stood next to the happy couple, still with blackish circles around his eyes, still sort of glaring at the world.

Guyan smiled at the sight of them all. He waved. Kaden and Jerry happily waved back. Rob only nodded, tersely. Guyan grinned at him.

"Now, don't poke at the raccoon!" Aiyana scolded, grinning also.

"Why not?" Guyan asked, with a big show of innocence, widening his eyes.

Aiyana chuckled, and elbowed him. She had so much to learn and do, now! Meeting his family would happen today! And learning to dance, finding her own family. She was now working with Guyan, to help spirits cross over happily, and openly. A new language would also have to be learned. So much! But she had the most wonderful teacher and partner. She leaned against him and he put his arm around her, as they watched the Grand Entry together.

About the Author

Penel j Smith is a physically disabled author and artist. She wrote and illustrated the children's book <u>Hugo and Fluffy Tales</u>. It is dedicated to H.H. The Dalai Lama, with permission from his assistant, Tsultrim Dorjee.
A copy of <u>Hugo and Fluffy Tales</u> was presented to H.H. The Dalai Lama, and he enjoyed the book.
Penel also wrote an ebook of humorous short stories and poems, <u>Servant and Several Sillinesses</u>. The short story, "Servant" tells the story of Kitzi's romance.
She has had poems published in an anthology along with Nik Beat. And also had a poem published in India.

As stated in the apology, Penel has often been seen as Indigenous. Once, a man at Na-Me-Res in Toronto asked her what Tribe she was from. When she replied that she was not Indigenous, he said, "Oh, you <u>pass</u> for White!" in a sarcastic voice. Since then, she usually says, "I don't know" if asked.

A funny incident happened at the Powwow during the Pan Am Games in Toronto. Penel got up to dance when all there were invited. She found her seat taken when she stopped. A white woman offered her a seat, because of Penel's cane. Then the woman said very loudly to her friends, "I gave up my seat to a REAL Indian!!!" Penel did not correct her.